IF YOU LOVED ME

Other Titles in the

True-to-Life Series from Hamilton High

by Marilyn Reynolds:

Baby Help

Too Soon For Jeff

Detour for Emmy

Telling

Beyond Dreams

But What About Me?

IF YOU LOVED ME

True-to-Life Series
from Hamilton High

By Marilyn Reynolds

Morning
Glory
Press

Buena Park, California

Library of Congress Cataloging-in-Publication Data

Reynolds, Marilyn, 1935-
    If you loved me / by Marilyn Reynolds.
        p.   cm. -- (True-to-life series from Hamilton High)
    Summary: Racially mixed seventeen-year-old Lauren,
the daughter of drug users, is pressured to have sex with her
boyfriend and questions her promise to herself to stay a virgin
until she is married.
        ISBN 978-1-885356-54-3 (1-885356-54-4) (hc.)
        ISBN 978-1-885356-55-0 (1-885356-55-2) (pbk.)
        [1. Sexual abstinence Fiction. 2. Sexual ethics Fiction. 3.
High schools Fiction. 4. Schools Fiction. 5. Drug abuse Fiction. 6. Racially mixed people Fiction.] I. Title. II. Series:
Reynolds, Marilyn, 1935-   True-to-life series from Hamilton
High.
        PZ7.R3373If   1999
        [Fic]--dc21
                                                                99-29522
                                                                CIP

MORNING GLORY PRESS, INC.
6595 San Haroldo Way   Buena Park, CA 90620-3748
    714/828-1998, 1-888/612-8254   FAX 714/828-2049
                e-mail mgpress@aol.com
        Web Site http://www.morningglorypress.com
        Printed and bound in the United States of America

"This would be a perfect time — the whole house to ourselves, no one to interrupt us, no gear shifts or steering wheels to maneuver around . . . I'll take care of everything. You know I won't hurt you."

I look out the window, watch lights go off in the house across the street, wonder what to say.

"But I promised myself . . ."

"I know. I know all about your promise. But you were a kid, then. You're not a kid anymore."

"But I . . ."

Like Marilyn Reynolds' other novels,
If You Loved Me is part
of the **True-to-Life Series from Hamilton High.**
Hamilton High is a fictional, urban, ethnically mixed
high school somewhere in Southern California.
Characters in the stories are imaginary
and do not represent specific people or places.

ACKNOWLEDGMENTS

For their close readings and critical comments on this work in progress, I wish to thank:

Dale Dodson, Cindi Foncannon, Karen Kasaba, Judy Laird, Karyn Mazo-Calf, Mike Reynolds, Matt Reynolds, Sharon Reynolds-Kyle, and Anne Scott.

Lisa Lundstrom at Calvine High School.

Marc Mallinger and student readers at South County Community School.

Barry Barmore and student readers at Century High School.

Marilyn Reynolds

To Sharon, Cindi, and Matt

CHAPTER

1

The sun is barely up when I meet Tyler at the rickety old bench under the palm tree at the north end of the Hamilton High School parking lot.

"Hey, Curly," he says, giving me a quick kiss.

We squeeze hands three times, meaning "I love you," and walk together into the B building. I like the early morning quiet of Hamilton High, with only a few students on their way to zero period classes.

We're about five minutes early, so, except for Mr. Harper, we're the first to arrive at creative writing. Mr. Harper, also known as "The Harp," because he's always harping on us to write more, is staring off into space. He is cradling his grungy coffee cup, warming his hands. He looks as if he's just rolled out of bed, stubble-faced and sleepy-eyed.

"Good morning, Teacher," Tyler and I say in a sing-songy, kindergarten sort of way.

The Harp groans and pours more coffee into his cup from a thermos that probably hasn't been washed since he started teaching here five years ago.

Tyler and I take seats next to each other and get out our notebooks. Blake comes dragging in, clutching a coffee cup. He's wearing thrift store corduroy pants, dark brown, and a wrinkled white T-shirt with a picture on the front of an old guy soaking in a bathtub filled with mud. "Take a bath" it says, in big mud-colored letters across the back. Except for Coach Howard, who's so old he can give an eyewitness account of the landing of the Mayflower, Blake's the only guy at Hamilton High who wears brown corduroy pants from the seventies.

"Your mommy sure dressed you funny this morning," Tyler says. Blake just smiles the sweet smile that lights his pudgy face. He sits down on the other side of Tyler and holds out a handful of seeds. Tyler looks closely, then extends his hand. Blake dumps the seeds and sits back, looking self-satisfied. Tyler looks even more closely, holds one up to the light, then puts it in his mouth and bites down.

"Tangerine," Tyler says. "I'm pretty sure."

"How do you know it's not an orange seed? Or lemon?" Blake says, frowning.

"I *don't* know for sure. It's just what I think. I'm right, huh?"

Blake takes a dollar from his pocket and hands it to Tyler.

So far, in the seed identification bet, Tyler's ahead by twelve dollars. Tyler's been interested in plants since he was a little kid, and he knows a whole lot more than Blake can believe he knows.

They've made up certain rules — Blake can't bring any seeds that are poison, he has to gather the seeds himself, from local plants, and the seeds have to be at least an eighth of an inch long. Tyler has to identify the seeds when he gets them, not carry them around all day, or get help from the biology teacher.

Blake makes me laugh. He wants to bet on *everything*. In fact, in junior high school, his nickname was Betcha.

By the time the bell rings, all twelve creative writing students are in the room, seated, notebooks open.

"When I wake up, I want you to be ready to go, notebooks out, thinking caps on," The Harp hammered into us during the first week of school. "It's a privilege to be in this class. If you ever feel like it's just too, too very much for you to be ready to work when the bell rings, I'll quick-whisk a drop card up to officialdom." We pretty much take The Harp seriously, because we *want* to be here. Not like math, or geography. I mean, I suppose those things are important, to someone, but they're nap time for me.

By the last reverberation of the tardy bell, The Harp is standing in front of his desk, eyes wide open, shoulders back, alive.

"Okay. Let's get started. Here's our jumping off sentence for the autobiography assignment," he says, handing out quarter-sheets of paper with the photocopied sentence.

When we all have the paper in our hands he reads, "You don't know about me without you have read a book by the name of *The Adventures of Tom Sawyer*, but that ain't no matter."

"Huck Finn," Zack calls out from the back of the room where he's trying to get the printer to work.

"No brainer," Tyler says.

"It was the best of times, it was the worst of times," Zack yells.

"*Tale of Two Cities,*" three people yell back.

"Double no brainer!" Tyler yells. "How about 'That Sam I Am. That Sam I Am. I do not like that Sam I Am.'"

We all laugh, including Mr. Harper, who then leans against his desk in his relaxed teacher pose and says, "Remember, this is creative writing, not creative talking, so . . ."

He arches one eyebrow practically to the ceiling and surveys the classroom with the smile that makes me think he knows a secret. Most of the girls at Hamilton High have crushes on Mr. Harper. I did, too, when I was a sophomore, but that was before Tyler Bronson. Tyler Bronson and me, Lauren Bailey. Bronson and Bailey. We're a pair.

" . . . if you could just pay attention long enough to hear your assignment . . . ?" Harper says over the hum of the classroom. He waves one of the quarter-sheets of paper in the air, over his head. "The part I want you to concentrate on, and write from, is 'You don't know me without . . .' I want you to THINK about it — not doodle it while you're watching reruns of 'Beavis and Butthead,' or mumble it over and over again while you're staring into space. THINK about what it is that people can't know you without. For instance, *you* don't know *me* without you know I teach English to the hope of the nation. And you also don't know me without you know that I am working on a novel of epic proportions."

"Am I going to be in your novel, Mr. Harper?" Kelsey says, batting her thick, lengthy lashes.

"I'm only on page 3,247, Kelsey. I can't tell yet. So far you're not . . . Zack?"

"How long does this have to be?"

Mr. Harper sighs. "You're *writers*. It's as long or as short as it needs to be, given what you're writing . . . Now, what is it for *you* that people *must* know, or they can't know *you*? Start with the phrase, 'You don't know me without . . .' and continue on from there."

"Mr. Harper?" Shawna asks.

We all turn to look at Shawna, sitting in her chosen place in the far back corner of the room. Shawna is this mystery person who keeps her head down so you can never see her face. She's in my peer communications class, too, and it's the same way there. She sits in the back of the room and hides under her hair. Blake and I have a bet to see who can be the first to find out what color Shawna's eyes are. We've had the bet since school started, and neither of us has had a chance to see Shawna's eyes.

Right now, Shawna is facing The Harp, but her hair is down over her face so you can't even see her mouth, much less her eyes.

"Yes, Shawna?" The Harp says, the look on his face revealing that he is as surprised to hear from her as the rest of us are.

"Do we have to tell the truth?"

"Well, as you know, autobiography *is* generally considered to be nonfiction."

"So we have to tell the truth?" she says, pushing for a concrete answer with more words than she's ever before spoken aloud in class.

"You don't have to stick to the facts, but you have to tell the truth," Mr. Harper says.

"What does *that* mean?"

Harper looks at Shawna and sighs.

"It means it can be *creative* nonfiction. And, by the way, I hope you're all started on a book in the autobiography category by now. Reading and writing, two sides of the same coin. Right?"

For once I'm ahead in the assignment. I'm more than halfway through an autobiography, *Angela's Ashes*, and I can hardly put it down. Really, this book is the reason I'm behind in my English class assignments. It's way more interesting than *Jane Eyre*.

"Let's take about five minutes to do a quick outline, or cluster ideas, before you start on your first draft."

In the middle of a page of notebook paper, I write, "You don't know me without . . ." and draw a circle around the statement. An avalanche of things slides through my brain. I draw a bunch of lines extending from the circle, like spokes on a wheel. Next I label the lines as fast as I can: Born drug addicted. Dead mother. I LOVE TYLER. Only fam — Gram. No to drugs. Yes to staying a virgin. Mixed race. Baby on the trail. Dad dead or alive? There's so much! Where will I start?

As if he's read my mind, Harper says, "I'm not asking for a full length autobiography here. Try to narrow things down to the core of you — the essence of you. I probably *can* know you without knowing you had the mumps in the third grade."

"I don't like the way that opening sentence sounds," Tyler says.

"You, Tyler Bronson, are criticizing the opening sentence of one of America's greatest novels?" Harper asks.

"Not criticizing it in *Huck Finn*, exactly. I just don't like it for myself."

Harper smiles. "That's what I love about teaching creative writing. You have opinions. Anybody else want to express an opinion?"

"It sounds weird to me, too," Blake says.

"Weird?" Harper says.

"You know. It doesn't sound like anything anyone *I* know would ever say."

"Okay," Harper says. "You've got a point. Huck speaks in a particular dialect, as does Jim. They're not dialects *we* hear or speak. Change the wording but keep the idea. Okay?"

"How should we change it?" Zack asks.

"Ay!" Harper says, running his hand through his hair. "*You* have to decide. Keep the original wording if you want, I don't care as long as it makes sense."

There's a buzz in the classroom, but it's obvious Harper is through with questions. He sets the timer for fifteen minutes, like he does every day, and we all, Harper included, start writing. "Quick-Write," it's called, because we're supposed to write as fast as we can, without self-editing, or self-censorship. That part comes later, after the first few drafts.

What *is* at the core of me, I wonder? I jot down ideas from the subjects I've clustered. First there's Tyler Bronson, who is my one true love. And the thing is, the miracle really, is that he loves me, too. Since the day we met, he's been there for me whenever I needed him. And I'm there for him, too. He's helping me learn not to sweat the small stuff, and I'm helping him learn to appreciate his mother. And we both help each other with our creative writing projects.

I glance over at him at the same time he's checking me out. He gives me that white-toothed, dimpled, light-up-the-room smile, then turns back to his paper. He is tan, from working in the sun. His arms are covered with a soft, golden down. I think of running my hand lightly over his arm, barely touching the downy hairs. I'm melting.

I guess my meltdown is somehow felt across the room,

because The Harp looks up from his paper, right at me, and taps his pen — a sign that I should be writing rather than melting. After a quick rereading of the assigned sentence, I decide to change the word "without" to "unless." To my modern ear that sounds better.

I tackle the mother spoke of the wheel of me:

> *You don't know me unless you know my mother was a big time druggie. She's dead now. I guess that's pretty important if you're going to know me. My mother'd been doing speed all the time she was pregnant with me. The first thing I had to do as a person in the world was get through drug withdrawal. So right off, the doctor turned me over to a social worker, who turned me over to a foster mom. I don't even know who that person was, the one who rocked me when I was all jumpy and kept me warm when I got the shivers, and got me to eat when all I wanted was a jolt of speed. I've probably got a damaged brain because of all that. My gramma says she's sure my brain works fine, but, like in math? Sometimes I just don't get it.*

I feel the familiar anger rising within me as I write about my mother. Often, when people first hear that my mother's dead, they look all sad, and they say stuff like, "Oh, I'm so sorry." But *I'm* not sorry. It's lucky for me she's dead.

I don't want to keep writing about the mother stuff. If I think about her very long I accumulate a load of anger that rushes to spill all over the place. But the only place I want to let that anger out is on the volleyball court. I get power from it in my serves, and in my spikes, and then I lock it back in its compartment until the next game.

I'm not stupid. I know that if a person lets anger eat at them, they lose a lot of the good stuff in life. Besides, maybe you *can* know me without knowing what a rotten person my mother was.

I go on to the mixed race spoke.

You don't know me unless you know I'm mixed race. On those forms where you're supposed to check the little boxes, there's never a box for me. White/Black/Chinese is not a combination they include, but that's what I am. White on my mom's side and my dad was half black and half Chinese. At least that's what Grams tells me. I wouldn't know. My dad may be dead by now, too. Anyway, he's dead to me.

Grams tells me I'm a beautiful mongrel, and that when the whole world gets all mixed up, like I am, we'll all be better off. She says there can't be racial prejudice when the races are no longer distinct. That's my grams, always looking at the bright side. She's a big part of my life because without her I'd probably be shuffling through the system, going from one foster home to another, having to deal with who knows what.

The truth is, I like being a mix. That way no one can categorize me.

What else would a person need to know about me? I've got plans for my future. I already know I want to be some kind of writer — maybe books, but probably a journalist. I know I'll want a paycheck, so journalism's more of a sure thing.

I doodle some more, pull more stuff from the avalanche. My favorite color is purple. I'm afraid of snakes. I'm afraid people won't like me. I wish I had blonde hair like Amber instead of this dark, curly stuff.

I'm a Virgo, which is supposed to mean I'm methodical, talented and hard-working, and I stick with my long-term goals until I accomplish what I've set out to do. According to this astrology thing I read, it said my negative side was that I could become too tied to rules, and also I might be nagging, and critical. Maybe some of those things are true. I do have long-term goals. I don't think I'm nagging and critical, though. I asked Tyler about that once, if he thought I was nagging.

"No way," he said. "My mom's a classic nag, and you're not a thing like my mom."

Anyway, I don't really believe in astrology. My mother was a Virgo, too, and I know for sure I'm *nothing* like she was. All she cared about was drugs. I *hate* drugs and I hate anyone who uses them. It's such a stupid waste! What else? I have a highly developed sense of smell, which isn't always a good thing. Like once my gramma had this guy, Lloyd, who was sort of in love with her, but he was always letting little silent, sneaky farts. He thought no one knew, but I could smell him clear in the next room. I told my gram about it, and then it got so every time I caught his scent I'd get the giggles. Which would get Grams started. Poor Lloyd. He didn't last long at our house. He ended up marrying some woman he met in a bar. She was a chain-smoker, which was probably to Lloyd's advantage because she'd smoked away her sense of smell. But I suppose knowing about Lloyd is sort of like knowing about having mumps in the third grade — not too important.

Here's another thing that's *way* important, though, because it made me think seriously about my life. You don't know me unless you know my gram and I discovered a newborn baby, about two hours old, under a bush, up in the foothills. That totally changed the way I thought about certain things.

The timer goes off and it's as if I'm roused from a deep dream. At first I can't get my mind off that baby, all sticky and covered with dirt, a long, bloody cord, thick as a rope, still attached to its belly.

"What's something we can't know you without, Zack?" Harper asks.

"You can't know me without you know I have the mind of Einstein and the body of Hercules."

"Mmmmmm," Harper says, looking unimpressed.

"Conrad?"

"I have six older brothers."

"Yes . . . I can see that such a family dynamic would definitely be a major factor in one's life," Harper says.

"Lauren?"

I glance at the spokes of my circle. I'm embarrassed to talk about how much I love Tyler. And the business with my mother, the dead druggie? That's kind of private. My good friends know, like Tyler, and Amber, but it's not exactly the kind of thing I want to announce to a whole classroom. And everybody knows about the baby discovery 'cause it was front page news in the *Hamilton Daily Times* for weeks.

My face is growing hotter and hotter as everyone sits waiting for me to answer Mr. Harper's question. I scan my paper one more time.

"I'm a Virgo?" I manage to squeak out.

Everyone laughs, or groans, except Kelsey.

"Wow! Really? Me, too," she says, as if she's gained new respect for me.

"Okay, okay," Harper says. "Remember how when you were first learning to swim it was terribly frightening to put your face in the water? And then to float like that? Head submerged? That's how this topic is. It takes courage to go below the surface, but you can't get anywhere without doing it."

CHAPTER

2

Hanging around talking with Tyler after creative writing doesn't make for getting to first period on time. I rush through the door to peer communications just as the tardy bell rings. Ms. Woods glances at me but doesn't say anything.

Zero period and first I've got the two best classes, and the two coolest teachers, at Hamilton High. After first period? Things get pretty blah.

I take my seat behind Amber, who waves her hand back at me without turning around. I reach out, stick my hand in front of her face and wave back. She turns and smiles.

Amber is my best friend in the whole world, except for Tyler. They're different friendships, though. I mean, *Amber's* the kind of friend who I couldn't care less how I look when I see her, and I can say whatever I want without worrying that she'll think I'm stupid.

When we were nine years old, we decided to become blood sisters. I think we'd seen it in some old movie, maybe "Stand By Me," where these kids, boys, decide to be blood brothers. Anyway, one day when Amber was at my house, we got into

Grams' first-aid drawer and found the needle she always used to get splinters out with. Grams was out pruning roses, or planting flowers, or some garden kind of thing, and we knew she'd be outside for a long time.

We took the book of matches from the drawer and I lit a match and held it to the needle's end, to sterilize it, the way I'd seen Grams do. My hand was all shaky because I knew Grams would go ballistic if she found me with a lit match. After just a few seconds I blew out the match and waited until it was cool enough to touch, then dropped it into the waste-basket. Then we took the needle into the kitchen and sat close to each other at the kitchen table. I sat holding the needle, staring at it.

Finally, Amber, who's the bravest about seeing blood, took the needle from me and started poking herself on the tender inside of her left wrist, until little drops of blood surfaced. Then she handed me the needle.

"Hurry up, before I stop bleeding," she'd said.

I took the needle and scratched gently at my wrist. Nothing happened.

"Harder!" she said, squeezing her wrist, getting a tiny bit more blood up. "Hurry!"

I stuck myself harder and I must have hit a vein or something because blood started oozing out. The sight of it made me feel sick. But Amber quick put her wrist over mine and we said the words we'd already memorized.

"On my honor, I promise to always be there for you, for better or worse, and to always be honest and true. And the more we get together, the happier we'll be."

Looking back, I can see that our blood sister promise was kind of a combination between the Brownie pledge and marriage vows, but it meant a lot to us then and it still does.

After our ritual, we went to the bathroom and found band-aids. My wrist was still bleeding but Amber assured me it was nothing. She put a band-aid on tight and made me promise not to look for two days.

"Okay, Sister Blondie," I told her.

"Okay, Sister Kinky," she said.

Those were our secret names for each other, chosen because of our hair. But we never used the whole names in front of anyone else. Amber was S.B. and I was S.K. Which was fine, until one day Amber's mom heard me call her S.B. and thought I'd said S.O.B., which meant we couldn't play together for a month.

"**L**auren? Are you with us?" Ms. Woods — Woodsie — asks.

"Now I am," I say, wondering if this is the first time she's said my name. Sometimes I get totally lost in a daydream, or a memory, like just now, when I was thinking about the old days with Amber. Usually I don't daydream in peer communications though, because it's almost always interesting. I sit up straight, ready to pay attention.

"Okay. Let's do a little brainstorming here," Woodsie says. "For the next several weeks, we'll be exploring current issues that affect us all. We'll bring in guest speakers, you'll do projects, we'll develop useful lists of resources such as counseling services and hot lines . . . Now, what issues face you, as young people, and all of us, as a society?"

Woodsie waits at the chalkboard, chalk in hand, ready to start writing.

Silence.

"Come on, now. I know it's early. Even so, I'll bet you're aware of at least one issue that needs work. Scott?"

If I were a teacher, which I plan never to be, I'd call on Scott, too. He *always* has an answer.

"AIDS," he says.

Woodsie writes AIDS on the board.

"Asshole cops," Mark, a skater, calls from the back of the room.

Woodsie stands with chalk poised, not writing.

"Mark, might you think of a way to rephrase that so if my

uncle, who's a police officer, happens to visit, he won't be insulted by a stereotype?"

"That's what they *are!*" Mark says.

"How about police brutality?" Amber says.

That's something I forgot to say about Amber earlier. She hates conflict, so she's always trying to get people to agree.

Woodsie writes "police brutality" on the board.

"Whatever," Mark says.

Finally, the class gets warmed up and people are shouting out topics faster than Woodsie can write. Teen pregnancy; drunk driving; gangs; homelessness; gay rights; school violence; Dr. Kevorkian; kids who do drugs . . .

"Parents who do drugs," Shawna calls out from behind her hair.

We end up with a list of more than twenty issues.

"Mark, could you copy these topics from the board for me? Then we can get duplicates made for everyone."

Mark gives Woodsie a look that indicates he'd rather eat kitty litter, but he takes out a sheet of paper and starts writing. Woodsie kills me, the way she gets everyone involved. Mark's already been kicked out of the math class for defiance of authority, but here Woodsie's got him doing a teacher pet kind of thing.

When Mark's finished with the paper, Woodsie brings it to me and says, "Would you take this to the office and get thirty copies, please, Amber?"

Amber and I both look at her a bit strangely. Woodsie slaps her forehead with the palm of her hand.

"Oh, no! I've done it again!" she says, with an embarrassed laugh.

Amber and I laugh, too, then I take the paper and go to the office where the line for the copier is about a mile long.

The funny thing is, a lot of people get me and Amber mixed up. It's not unusual for someone I don't know very well to call me Amber. And people sometimes call her Lauren. That is *so* weird. Because I've got my black dad's dark, curly hair, dark eyes, and full lips (which I like). And Amber has straight blond hair, and blue eyes, and really thin lips (which she hates). We both have dimples in our chins. That's about it. Well, I guess we have similar tastes. We trade clothes back and forth, but still, no way do we look alike.

Tyler says people get us mixed up because we're always together and we have a lot of the same mannerisms. Amber pulls at her hair when she's thinking, and so do I. And we both put our hands on our hips when we're irritated. I never even knew that. Tyler pointed it out to me one day, when I was complaining about how the substitute volleyball coach had called me Amber.

I get back to class with copies of the list just as the passing bell rings.

"Thank you, LAUREN," Ms. Woods says with a smile.

Turning toward Amber she says, "See you tomorrow, AMBER."

We both laugh.

On our way to English, I ask Amber why she'd missed volleyball practice yesterday.

"Coach Terry practically had a seizure about how one person missing a practice lets the whole team down. Really, I thought I was going to have to hold her down and use a tongue depressor."

Amber laughs, but not like her heart's in it.

"I couldn't go," Amber says.

"She was mad at *me* because I'm your friend. Like it was *my* fault you weren't there and why couldn't I just magically produce you."

"Sorry," Amber says.

"Why weren't you there? We *do* need you."

"I know. It's just . . ."

I keep waiting for her to finish the sentence, but she turns away from me and I realize she's about to cry.

"Hey. Amber? What's wrong? It's not that big a deal — just

one practice," I say.

"It's not that."

"Well, what then?"

She's got big tears gathering in her eyes and I know things are serious because Amber never cries. I was with her when she fell off the play structure and broke her arm, back in the fifth grade. She didn't even cry then — she just gritted her teeth until the nurse came, and then she said, all calm, "This hurts bad."

"C'mon," I tell her. "I'll buy you a cinnamon bun."

She nods and we walk away. Hamilton High is supposed to be a tightly closed campus, but there's this one wimpy security guy, Homer, who guards the back gate but who takes any excuse from any girl.

"My friend has terrible cramps," I tell him, and he opens the gate.

We walk the three blocks to Carole's Coffee Shoppe without talking. I know from our years of friendship that Amber will tell me what's bothering her, but I can't be pushy about it. I order two small cappuccinos and a huge cinnamon bun and take them to the table where Amber sits staring out the window.

"We shouldn't be cutting class," she says. "I'll be grounded for months if my mom finds out."

"I know," I say, thinking about how Mr. Snyder is already mad at me because I hadn't finished the *Jane Eyre* reading assignment for Friday.

"I never thought anything like this would happen to me," Amber says.

"Like what?"

"This herpes stuff."

"I thought it was gone. That was months ago, wasn't it?"

She nods her head. The tears are flowing full on now.

"It doesn't really ever go away. It just hides out for a while. And then, when you think everything's okay, it comes back."

"But, you haven't done anything . . . been with anyone . . .?"

"See, that's the thing," she says, wiping her eyes. "I can be celibate for the rest of my life, and I'll still have herpes."

She wipes at her nose now, too. I go to the counter, pick up a handful of extra napkins, and give one to her.

"Yesterday, in sixth period, I started feeling this tingling ache in my . . . you know, down there," she says, kind of half-nodding downward. "And my butt felt fiery and my legs hurt. I knew I had to get home, into a hot, baking soda bath. But God, why me? I only had sex once, and with a clean guy, too. At least, I thought he was a clean guy. And now I've got this herpes curse for the rest of my whole life. I should have stayed a virgin. Like you."

Amber wipes her nose and eyes again, still crying. Blake comes in, as usual at this time of day. He says it's against his principles to attend P.E. classes. Noticing us, Blake starts over to our table. Then he gets a good look at Amber and goes back to his usual spot at the counter, where he sits watching the street, jotting notes in his journal — observations of life, he says, whenever anyone asks.

I turn my attention back to Amber.

"They'll probably find a cure for herpes pretty soon," I say.

"Don't be stupid!"

Amber's tone is so angry, I don't know whether to stay or go. I sit rearranging the little packets of fake sugar in their green glass container. After a while, sort of a long while, really, Amber tells me she's sorry.

"It all seems so unfair to me. I've got this stuff for life, and it can just flare up whenever it wants to. Like right now, no way can I play volleyball until it's under control again."

"I don't get what it's got to do with volleyball," I say.

"Yeah, well, I don't want to go into a lot of nasty detail about oozing sores in private places, but trust me, it's gross. It hurts to pee and I have to keep putting on this ointment stuff. And my mom wants to know why I'm taking five baths a day. Can you imagine me telling my Sunday School teacher mom, "Oh, I bathe a lot because it soothes my STD?"

Amber shakes her head and starts crying again.

"Didn't they tell you the outbreaks are usually less frequent after the first year?"

"Yeah, but you know what? I'll always have it, whether it's acting up or not. And if I have a baby, it could be blind, or retarded, because of herpes."

With this Amber puts her head down on the table and lets out huge, heaving sobs. A few people look at us, then glance away. I catch Blake looking at us once, but then he quick looks back down at his notebook. He better not be writing about us!

I pull my chair around the table, close to Amber, and rub her back. I don't know what else to do.

It was stupid of me to tell her maybe there'd soon be a cure. She's got to deal with how things are *now*, and with how there may never be a real cure. I feel so sorry for her *I* get all teary eyed. I don't think she deserves this. It's not like she's some sex-crazed slut.

Amber raises her head. She wipes her eyes and nose with the last of the napkins. Her eyes are red and swollen.

"Thanks, S.K." she says, giving me a weak smile.

"For what?"

"You know. For listening. For not walking out on me when I said you were stupid. For caring enough to cut class."

"You'd do the same for me, S.B. That's what I know."

I guess it's kind of silly, high school seniors calling each other by secret initials. But it's what we've been doing since we were nine, and it reminds us of how we're always there for one another. When we're thirty, I think we'll still be S.K. and S.B. to each other. I hope so, anyway.

CHAPTER

3

"**K**eep the pressure on! Don't let up!" Coach Terry yells from just outside the volleyball court where she paces back and forth, five feet one way, five feet back.

"If we're going to beat Hacienda Hills we've got to stay aggressive. Everyone! Pretend you're Lauren!" she yells.

"You never let up," she told me once. "I wish all of my players had your heart."

Coach Terry doesn't know where I get my power, though. It's not heart. It's the power of anger. The volleyball is my mother — Every time she comes close to me I jam her over the net. Hard. Spike her down to the ground. Hard. Serve her at top speed. Hard. For what she did to me. For what she didn't do for me. For loving drugs instead of loving me. For the hurt and rejection I still feel, no matter how far down I bury it. When she comes flying high overhead, I leap upward, arms stretched long, fists closed. POW! She's down. Bystanders cheer.

"Amazing strength," some say. "Great control of the ball." But it's not the ball I'm controlling. It's my druggie mother.

I don't tell anyone where I get my power. It sounds too crazy.

But *I* know where it comes from and I use it whenever I step onto the court. When I step off the court, I leave it behind, except for those times I get thinking about things. Like in today's writing assignment.

After volleyball practice I shower away the sweat, and grime, and anger. Then I drive to Greener Nursery and Fountains, where Tyler works, and sit in the car, waiting for him to come out. Everyone who works here wears red and white checked shirts and bib overalls, like they're supposed to be farmers. Too much! But Tyler likes working here because he loves plants and gardens. He plans to be a landscape architect, and he's learning a lot from Mr. Schaefer.

Shawna, the girl from creative writing who never shows her eyes, works here, too. Tyler says she's different at work, more relaxed. I tried to get him to check out the color of her eyes, so I could win my bet with Blake, but he says that would be cheating. Really, Tyler's got to be about the nicest, most honest guy in the whole universe. Sometimes I can hardly believe he loves *me* — like what are the chances of having something that good happen?

Greener Nursery is where I first met Tyler. I'd seen him at school. He's one of those guys that girls notice, but he doesn't even know they're noticing him. Anyway, on this one Saturday about a year ago, Grams asked me to go to the nursery with her, to pick up some "autumn color." Well, my social calendar being a complete blank, I said sure, I'd go along. Lucky for me, because when we got there, Tyler was the one who waited on us.

He led the way to the pansies.

"I think I'll use mostly whites and purples with a touch of pink for the garden this season. What do you think, Lauren?"

What I thought was I wished I could say something clever, to impress Tyler. But what I actually said was, "Okay." How weak!

Tyler pulled out the best plants in white and deep purple and put them on a cart.

"We just got some Mexican sage. That's got a great purple stalk. It's hearty and it would give you some height variation with the pansies," Tyler said, leading the way back past a big, gurgling fountain, to the area of drought-resistent plants.

Tyler pulled off a sprig of sage, rubbed it between his palms, then held it out for Grams to smell.

"Delightful!" she said.

Tyler beamed. Then he held it out for me to smell. I took a big whiff and sneezed all over his hand. He and Grams both laughed while I fought the urge to drown myself in the fountain.

When we were finished choosing all the new plants, there wasn't room for everything to fit in Grams' Toyota.

"We deliver, you know," Tyler said.

"Oh, I know. But I always want to take things right home and get started," Grams told him.

"No charge," Tyler said.

So Grams agreed to have the plants delivered and she and I drove home empty handed.

"What a nice boy," Grams said.

I said nothing, still totally embarrassed by my ill-timed, ill-placed sneeze.

"He was quite taken with *you*, I noticed."

"Oh, puhleeze," I said, in my most sarcastic tone. "He didn't even look at me, except when I sneezed."

Grams laughed.

"It's not funny! It's soooo embarrassing!"

"Oh, come on. It was a sneeze, not a fart," Grams said, laughing even harder.

"At least I'm not like Lloyd," I said.

The thought of Lloyd got me laughing, too. I couldn't help it.

When we finally stopped laughing, Grams said, "That boy was looking at you most of the time, just not when you looked at him," Grams said.

"He's probably never seen such a weird creature," I said.

My grandma got all serious. "You're a beautiful young woman," she said.

"You think that 'cause you're my grandmother."

"No, I think that because I have eyes to see. Beauty's not as important as some other things about you. You've got a good heart, and you're dependable, and smart. But make no mistake, you're knock-em-dead beautiful, too."

Sometimes my grandma exaggerates.

Back to that Saturday, though. Grams and I had only been home for a few minutes when Tyler came driving up in a Greener Nursery and Fountains truck. Guess what color? Yep. Grassy green. I watched from the dining room window as he got out and came up the porch steps to the door. He rang the bell and stood back, checking out the potted plants that lined the front porch.

"Lauren! Could you get that please?" Grams called from the back.

"Yeah, could you, Lauren?" Tyler called from the front.

So I left my spying place and went to the door.

"Where do you want me to leave the plants?" Tyler asked.

He flashed that double-dimpled smile of his at me and my stomach got all fluttery. I always thought when love hit, it was your heart that fluttered, but not with me. It was my stomach.

"Plants?" he said, his smile broadening.

"Let's take them back here," Grams said, rounding the corner of the house from where she'd been working in the backyard.

"In the back," I said, and started to go inside.

"Lauren?"

"How did you know my name?"

"That's what she's been calling you," he said, nodding in Grams' direction.

"Oh, yeah, duh," I said.

"Come help me with this stuff."

So I did, happy for an excuse to be near him. We unloaded flats of pansies and four Mexican sage plants, and lots of purple and pink primroses.

"I brought some heather, too," Tyler told Grams. "I know you didn't buy it, and I can take it back, but I thought it would fit with the colors you were talking about planting."

"You're a genius," Grams said.

It turned out we needed more planting mix, so I rode back with Tyler to pick some up.

"I can take my lunch break now," Tyler said, after we loaded the planting mix and plants for another delivery onto the truck.

We got sodas at the drive-thru Jack-in-the-Box on the way back, and Tyler got chicken pieces and fries. Then we parked under a tree and I drank my soda while Tyler ate his lunch. I'd never been able to talk with a guy without feeling all self-conscious, maybe because I didn't have any brothers or sisters and grew up as sort of a loner. But it was different with Tyler. From the very beginning we talked as if we'd known each other forever.

When we got back to the house Grams was still planting. We unloaded the planting mix.

"Would you like some iced tea? Or lemonade?" Grams asked us.

"I've got to make another delivery," Tyler said.

"Well . . . I'd like to call your boss and tell him how helpful you've been. Would you mind?"

"No problem," Tyler said, his face turning a primrose shade of pink.

I walked with him back to the truck.

"Can I call you tonight?" he said.

"No problem," I said. Luckily, with my dark complexion, no one can tell whether I'm blushing or not.

When I went back to help Grams finish planting she took one look at me and said, "I told you so."

"Told me what?" I asked, all innocent.

"He likes you," she said. "And from the look on your face, you like him, too."

I didn't say anything, just kept digging, but we both knew she was right.

So that was it. Tyler and I've been together every day since that Saturday. We've got a big, one year anniversary coming up next month. That's from our first real kiss. The one that let us both know something important was going on between us.

After waiting for what seems a long time, I spot Tyler at the far end of the parking lot, unloading about a ton of baby plants into the trunk of a big, silver-gray Mercedes. I walk closer to where he is, but stand back a bit until he's finished. Ms. Mercedes hands him something. He opens the car door for her, waves goodbye, then comes trotting over to me.

"Hi, Mr. Green Jeans," I say, poking at his overalls.

"Hi, Curly," he says, running his hand over my hair.

"How're things on the farm?"

"Don't kick it," he says, flashing a five at me. "I like carrying supplies to the luxury car crowd."

"You want me to pick you up when you get off tonight?" I ask, knowing his car is without a battery until he gets paid.

"That'd be cool. I don't get off until ten, though. We're shifting our summer/fall stuff out of the interior section, making room for Christmas."

"That's okay. Grams'll let me keep the car out until eleven."

Tyler gives me a quick hug and a kiss.

"See you at ten. Gotta go now."

He runs toward the nursery and I get back in Grams' car and drive home. As I turn into the driveway I see Grams up by the porch, cutting roses.

"Hi, Sweet Thing," she calls to me as I get out of the car lugging my backpack.

I dump my pack on the lawn and walk over to give Grams a peck on her soft, saggy cheek.

"How's your day?" she asks, the same question she always asks.

"Fine," I say, the same answer I always give.

She holds up a bouquet of roses. "Two Mr. Lincolns," she says, holding out the deep red ones, "and two President Kennedys."

"Is this the assassinated Americans bouquet?" I ask.

"Oh, oh," she says. "I'd better cut a couple of these Peace roses to balance things."

"Or toss in a Martin Luther King Jr. and stay with the theme." She laughs. Even though my grams is old, she gets things.

"I'm taking flowers to the book group tonight, instead of my usual spinach dip. I'm afraid I'm in a spinach dip rut."

"Must be messy," I say, following Grams up the steps of the porch and into the house.

"I told Tyler I'd pick him up after work tonight, but I guess you want the car, huh?"

"Betty's stopping by for me. I thought you might want the car later, and I'm right on her way."

"Thanks, Grams."

"And there's some of that leftover veggie stir-fry in the fridge, and rice, too."

"Okay," I say, hoping maybe there's still some pizza left from last week. Veggie stir-fry is my gramma's idea of helping me get my five-a-day fruit and vegetable portions. It's okay, but not two nights in a row.

"What book are you talking about in your group tonight?"

"I hate to tell you," she says, concentrating on stripping the lower leaves and thorns from the rose stems and arranging them in a ceramic vase.

"Now I'm curious. What *did* you read this time?"

I reach into the fridge, get out a Diet Coke and wait for Grams to answer. She keeps fooling with Mr. Lincoln and President Kennedy.

"Grams?"

"Oh, if you must know! We read *Vox*. It wasn't *my* idea."

"*Vox?*"

"It was Millie's idea. I swear to goodness, she's the oldest one in the group. She's *got* to be at least seventy-two. And whenever

it's her turn to choose a book she always chooses something
. . . well . . . sexy."

Grams takes the flowers out of the vase, drops a handful of
those little glass rock things in the bottom and starts over again.

"What's it about?"

I can't believe my gramma's blushing, but the back of her
neck is turning pink. I move to the end of the sink where I can see
her face. She *is* blushing.

"What's it about?" I repeat.

She lays the flowers back on the counter top and looks me
square in the eye.

"Phone sex," she says, then turns back to her flowers.

"Phone sex?"

"Yes. Phone sex. But if you want to know anything else you'll
just have to read the book yourself. It's ridiculous. It's not worth
talking about."

"You'll talk about it tonight, won't you?"

"Oh, I suppose. Ridiculous! A bunch of old grannies sitting
around sipping wine and talking about phone sex!"

"*You're* not an old grannie," I tell her.

"Oh, look at this hair — white as snow."

It's true her hair is white as can be, but even though she's sixty,
she works out at a gym three days a week, and walks four miles
on the days she doesn't work out.

"Just feel these muscles," I say, grabbing her biceps.

She flexes and it feels like there's iron beneath her wrinkled
skin. We both laugh.

"When it's your turn to choose you should have them read
this," I say, digging my library book out of my backpack and
handing it to her. She wipes her hands on the kitchen towel and
takes *Angela's Ashes* from me.

"You can read it when I'm through," I tell her. "I'll call and
renew it."

"I've heard good things about this," she says, handing it back
to me. "Anything'd be uplifting after *Vox* . . . Did you see Sally

when you were in there?"

"Yeah. I forgot to tell you. Sally told me to say hello for her."

Grams used to work at the library. She's not really a librarian, but she knows a lot about books. When my grampa died, before I was even born, she went to work for the Hamilton Heights Library System. She said it beat sitting around feeling sorry for herself.

"Well, I'll see Sally when I return *this* silly book tomorrow."

"I might like to read that *Vox* book," I say, kind of embarrassed.

"It's trash," she says, giving me a long look. "But you're welcome to it. I won't return it yet."

I'm supposed to be reading all this other stuff for school, like *Jane Eyre*, and seventy pages a week from my history text. Both cures for insomnia as far as I'm concerned. I don't even know if I want to read that *Vox* book or not. I mean, what exactly *is* phone sex, anyway? But if it's something that makes my gramma blush, it must be interesting.

The phone rings and I reach for it, hoping it's Tyler calling on his break. Instead it's Grams' friend, Betty. I hand the phone to her and go back to my room to start my homework.

Grams has this habit of walking around in the backyard with the clippers while she talks on the phone. I guess that's how most of the pruning gets done. I don't mean to eavesdrop but she's right outside my window, cutting away at the scraggly growth of baby limbs at the trunk of the pepper tree.

"Phone sex!" Grams says.

I have no idea what Betty says, but whatever it is gets a shriek of laughter from Grams.

"I can only imagine what Ray would have said if I'd told him, 'Let's do it by phone tonight, Honey.'" More shrieks of laughter.

"What is *wrong* with people these days that they don't know the difference between sex and a phone call?"

More laughing and then Grams moves back by the fence and I open my notebook.

4

When I finally get serious about starting my homework, after a glass of water, and then an apple, and then another glass of water, I turn to the math section of my notebook. It's best to get that out of the way first. I write my name at the top of a sheet of notebook paper, stare at examples of equations, look at the first problem, and go on to the creative writing assignment. Maybe Amber and I will do our math together after school tomorrow. It's not due until Wednesday. Why rush things?

I read what I wrote in class today. I'm pretty sure I don't want to write about my early life. That's all stuff I want to put behind me. But that's what I start writing about anyway, like I have no control.

"You don't know me unless you know how messed up the first five years of my life were," is how I start, and then the words rush out as if someone opened a secret door — all that stuff I try not to think about, because what good can it do? I write so fast my hand cramps up. I rub my hand, change pens, change writing positions, and start again, fast, just trying to keep up with the words that are flooding from my mind.

When I was born, I was all strung out on drugs and so was my mother, Marcia Bailey. I nearly died. Can you believe it? That a woman would do that to her own kid? Every Mother's Day I hear so much of that mother-love stuff I want to puke! The love of *my* mother would be enough to kill a person. (From here on I'm going to call my mother by her name, because every time I call her "mother" it makes me mad all over again.)

By the time Marcia was seventeen, the age I am now, she was on the streets, being a slut for drugs. Most of the time no one had the slightest clue about where she was living. I was already three months old before my gramma even knew I'd been born. When she found out about me, though, she got me out of foster care and took me home to live with her.

All the time Marcia was in prison she was writing to Grams, saying how she'd put drugs behind her and she couldn't wait to get out and take care of her little girl. She'd say how much she loved me and Grams, and how sorry she was for all she'd put us through. Grams says she meant it, but she was too weakened by drugs to carry through. I don't believe it. I think if Marcia'd loved me she'd have kept her promises. I used to read those letters over and over again, and when I'd get to the part where she promised to take such good care of me, I'd say out loud, to the ghost of Marcia, "You were a selfish, rotten mother." I've had a lot of conversations with Marcia's ghost, but none of them has been very satisfying.

When Marcia got out of prison she came to get me. She told Grams she was going to take me to Texas, to be with my dad. We'd be a family there. Grams tried to talk her out of it, but one day Marcia just up and left, taking me with her. No forwarding address. Grams says she prayed for me every day, and did all she knew to do to find me. She kept thinking she'd hear from Marcia, at Christmas, or on her birthday, but that never happened.

Looking through old pictures, like when Marcia was in high school, before she turned into a full-time druggie, she doesn't look familiar to me. Sometimes I think if by some miracle she were to walk into my room, right now, I wouldn't even recognize her. I have no pictures of her, or of me, from the time she took me away from Grams to the time she was gone from my life forever. I have no memories of her either, or from that time. Maybe I remember a loud, shattering bang, and searing heat, and someone grabbing me and running with me. But maybe I only dream it. Anyway, I got out before the house blew up.

The newspaper clipping from Amarillo, Texas, says Marcia and a bunch of others were manufacturing methamphetamines in a makeshift kitchen lab when the whole thing blew up on them. Four people, including Marcia, were killed. Some eyewitness thought he saw a black man running out of the house with a child in his arms, but he wasn't sure. I'd like to think it was my dad, carrying me to safety. He's black, so it *could* have been him. I'd like to think at least one of my parents cared enough to save my life.

In a way I guess the explosion was lucky for me. I know that sounds cold — like what killed Marcia was my good luck. But Marcia nearly killed me before I was even born, what with her drug use and all. And she nearly killed me again, when I was five. There were probably plenty of times in between, times I don't remember, when my life was in danger with her.

Here's what happened after the explosion, though. Somebody had pinned a tag to my shirt and printed: Please contact Frances Bailey, this girl's grandmother, in Hamilton, CA.

Then they'd left me in an unlocked car in a church parking lot. When the family who owned the car came out of church, there I was. They took me to the church office and called the police. The police called my gramma. She flew to Texas the next day and took me home with her.

That's what she says. I wish I could remember. Sometimes, it's like it's just hovering at the outside of my brain, a full memory of that time. Someday I might try to get hypnotized and see if that would help me remember. But if my memories are really awful, why put myself through that?

When Grams got me, I only weighed about thirty pounds, which is closer to the average weight of a three-year-old than a five-year-old. And, this is really gross, when they took me to the hospital in Texas to give me a check-up, my head was so full of lice that they shaved off all my hair. I do have a picture from that time — skinny, bald-headed, kind of slumped. I looked like one of those pictures you see in magazines that have a caption, "Only seventy cents a day can make all the difference in the world to little Carmen." Except I looked worse because I had no hair.

Suddenly I'm tired of that topic, even though I know there's more I could explain. Like how sometimes I feel jealous and sad when I see a normal family, where the mom and dad love their kids, and take good care of them. You know the kind — little Janie's preschool graduation picture is up on the wall, along with her baby pictures, and a picture taken on Santa's lap when she was three.

My gramma has pictures of me from when I was three months old until I was two. There's even one of me and my father, Jack, who came to see me a few times when Marcia was in prison. I don't remember that at all, but Grams says he told her he was going to come twice a month, but after five visits he stopped coming.

Grams doesn't know why he stopped. Maybe he got sent to jail too. She'd liked him though, from when she'd known him when he and Marcia first got together. She thought he'd be good for Marcia, but it turned out the other way around. Marcia pulled Jack down into the drug pit with her.

In my mind, just like I always think of my mother as Marcia, I think of my father as Jack. Neither of them deserves to be recognized as a parent. Marcia and Jack, that's all they are to me. Not Mother and Father, or Mom and Dad, none of that stuff that means protection, or love, or any of the good things about families.

There's another picture of me with Marcia, just after she got out of prison. And there are lots of pictures with me and Grams. Then there are all of those blank years when nobody cared enough to take my picture, or feed me right, or keep me clean, and then the pictures start again when I was five.

It's strange to me that my aunt Claudia turned out so good and my mom turned into a junkie. Why? Whenever I ask my gramma about it, she gets all sad and says she doesn't understand it either. Everything seemed to be going along just fine.

Then Marcia started hanging out with a different crowd. Her whole personality changed. Grams thinks that once Marcia tried drugs, she was lost. Like it changed her body chemistry, or something.

Grams is the only one who ever truly loved me, until Tyler. And I'm not even sure Tyler could love me the way Grams did, if I were bald-headed and lice infested.

As I read over what I've written, a white hot anger rises within me, escaping from the secret compartment — the one I try always to keep locked up, unless I'm on the volleyball court. From my collection of colored marking pens, I take a heavy black marker.

I scrawl all over my rough draft assignment, in big, bold letters, **"I hate you, Marcia Bailey! If you'd loved me, you'd have quit all the drugs and taken care of me! You didn't love me! I'm glad you're dead! You weren't a real mother! A real mother loves her children! I never had a mother! I hate you! I hope you're in Hell! Burning and burning and burning and burning!"**

I rip the pages out of my notebook and crumple them, tight. I throw them into the waste-basket, in a fury, then grab them out again, take them into the living room, throw them into the fireplace and set them on fire.

Watching them burn I think of my mother, burning in the kitchen. Burning in Hell. Serves her right, I think. Then the tears come. I can't stop them.

Harper said we should have the courage to go beneath the surface of things, but the muck below my surface isn't clear and sparkling clean, like a swimming pool. It's more like a dark, dirty, murky swamp, with snakes and alligators and menacing barracuda. I don't want to write about that. I'm afraid I'll be pulled under and then I'll never reach the surface again.

Back in my room I open my math book, but I can't concentrate. By nine-thirty I've only completed one math problem. Maybe my writing assignment should start, "You don't know me unless you know the math part of my brain is broken and can't be fixed."

I go into the bathroom, splash water on my face, brush my teeth, run a pick through my hair and put on Tyler's favorite flavor of lip blush, "Sweet Strawberry." I grab a sweatshirt and *Angela's Ashes*, and drive to Greener Nursery and Fountains.

Once there, I park around back and go inside Mr. Schaefer's old office. He has a new office up front now, since they remodeled, so Tyler uses the old office. It's where he keeps his records of some experimental stuff he's doing.

I turn on a light that's way too dim, then sit down on the ratty couch and start reading *Angela's Ashes*. The book is written by this guy, Frank McCourt, who grew up in Ireland in a family so poor that awful things happened to them. Twin boys died, and a little girl died, all because they couldn't afford medical care, or decent food, or even enough blankets.

On top of it all, the father was a drunk and even when he was working he usually drank up the money they needed for food. Frank McCourt doesn't seem to hate his father the way I hate Marcia, but *I* hate him, just hearing of him. They're two of a kind, both so selfish they won't even do what's right to take care of their children.

I hear the door creak and there's Tyler, standing in front of me, grinning. My gramma has a bunch of old LPs from the sixties. One song says something like whenever I see you, you make my heart smile. That's how I feel right now, seeing Tyler. My heart is smiling big time.

"Been here long?" he says, sitting down beside me.

"Just one chapter's worth," I tell him, holding up my book.

"Done your math homework yet?"

I shake my head.

"I don't get why you're working ahead for creative writing, a class you've already got an **A** in, and not doing homework in the class where you're barely getting a **D**."

"Don't start sounding like Grams."

Tyler laughs. "You're a crazy girl."

"And craazzyy for loooovinnnn' yooooou," I sing out in a Patsy Cline imitation. (That's from another of my Grams' LPs.)

Tyler puts his arm around me, pulls me toward him and kisses me. The tip of his tongue teases along my lips and I get the taste of a dissolved mint overcoming all but a hint of the onion he must have had on his hamburger at his dinner break.

He pulls back and grins at me. "Ummm. Sweet Strawberry. More." He shuts off the light and I lean forward for another kiss, this one longer, more ardent. Hatred of Marcia falls away from me, until all I know is love for Tyler.

After a moment, Tyler raises his hand to my chin and gently lifts it so we're eye to eye.

"Good news," he says. "I've got good news."

"What?"

"Another trip to Vegas coming up."

Tyler's parents have this thing about going to Las Vegas every chance they get. His mom likes to gamble, even more than Blake, it seems, and his dad likes the shows. *And* . . . Tyler and I like having his house all to ourselves.

"They're leaving Thursday — not coming home until Monday. Four whole days," he says. "Mom stopped in earlier this evening to pick up some of our special plant food mix. She told me they'd just made reservations at the Luxor."

"What about Parker?"

Parker is Tyler's nine-year-old brother, who's cute, but can be a terrible pest.

"Parker's going to Nana's this time."

Tyler moves his hand to the back of my neck, leans toward me, and kisses me on the mouth, long and serious.

"We're gonna have a great weekend," he whispers.

"We can make pizza," I say.

"We can make more than pizza," he says, kissing me again, moving his hand under my sweatshirt, under my not very tight sports bra. His touch is warm and gentle.

"Get closer," he whispers, stretching out on the couch and pulling me close against him. He takes my hand and guides it downward. I feel his hardness under his farmer's overalls.

Tires screech near us and we jump apart. Some near accident in the parking lot. The mood is broken.

We walk to Grams' car and I drive Tyler home. He lives in a section he refers to as Baja Heights. Up the hill from him is where the rich people live.

Where he lives is still called Hamilton Heights, but it's at the not-so-rich low end. Nice, though. In Tyler's neighborhood the houses are newer than my Grams'. We just live in Hamilton — no Heights, not even lower Heights.

I park at the curb a few doors down from the Bronsons' house, so Tyler's mom won't know he's home and come running out to talk to us. I mean, I like his mom a lot. I wish I had one like her. But still . . .

Tyler takes a deep breath and sighs. I'm pretty sure what he's going to start talking about. It's a topic he's been bringing up more and more.

"Lauren," he says, then pauses. "Listen, Lauren."

The car is filled with Tyler's intensity. I wait to hear what's next.

"This would be a perfect time — the whole house to ourselves, no one to interrupt us, no gear shifts or steering wheels to maneuver around."

I look out the window, watch lights go off in the house across the street, wonder what to say.

"I'll take care of everything. Condoms, foam. You know I won't hurt you. I'd never do anything to hurt you. Please," he says, then, again in a whisper, "Please. I love you so much. I need you so much."

He kisses me, then lays his head against my chest. I sit with my arms around him.

"But I promised myself . . ."

"I know. I know all about your promise. But you were a kid, then. You're not a kid anymore."

"But I . . ."

"Just think about it," he says. "Tell me you will at least think about it. It's making me crazy."

"Okay," I say.

"Okay," he says, giving me a gentle kiss on the cheek and getting out of the car.

Tyler turns back for our usual "love you" sign, the one I taught him after a sign language demonstration in peer communications. I sign "Love you" back to him, to his soft mouth and gentle eyes, and then I pull away from the curb.

Back home, I sit in my desk chair, in the dark, and swivel to face the half-open window that looks out on the backyard. It is very dark out tonight, with no moon or stars.

Even though I can see only vague shadows, I know what's there — the pepper tree groaning against the roof, the deck with wicker chairs and bright cushions, the bird feeders outside the window.

I sip hot tea, listening to the chirp of crickets and the rustling of leaves. It is a peaceful place. I heard somewhere that certain places are healing places and I think my gramma's backyard is like that.

When Grams first brought me home from Texas there wasn't even a bed in this room. There was a big table where she had laid out a giant jigsaw puzzle, and there was a stack of dusty Christmas decorations in the corner.

"It's just a junk room, but we'll fix it up," Grams had said. Then she found some blankets and a pillow and made a bed for me on the floor. She laid down next to me, her head resting beside mine on the pillow. There was a sound outside the window that made me tense, scared.

"Just listen," Grams had said. "It's a good sign that the owl is there tonight."

I listened to the soft hooting sound while Grams rubbed my back. "The owl knows everything is fine, or she wouldn't have come to our tree."

It was the first time I could remember feeling safe. No matter how old I get, I think the fresh cool air coming through my bedroom window will remind me of that time back when I was five, when I first felt safe.

It's strange how I remember all about that night when I first came from Texas to my gramma's house, but almost nothing from the time immediately before, with Marcia. Grams says sometimes our minds block painful stuff, and maybe the time before she brought me home from Texas hurts too much to remember.

For a long time I sit in the dark, listening, thinking about the past, thinking about Tyler and what I know he wants to have happen. I want that, too, in a way. But I'm determined to stay a virgin until I get married. True love waits. I hear that all the time and it makes sense to me.

Finally, I turn on the light and reach into my bottom drawer, my diary/journal drawer, and pull out the hand-tooled leather journal that has the number fourteen on the spine, embossed in gold.

I fan the pages, watching dust motes rise, then fall. I run my hand over the soft leather cover, then turn to page one, September 8, and reread what I wrote on my fourteenth birthday:

Dear Journal — A promise from me to me,
I promise not to do anything to mess my life up. No
DRUGS (like wrecked my parents)! No SEX (like wrecked
Sarah Mabry)
  NO DRUGS EVER.
  STAY A VIRGIN UNTIL MARRIAGE.

I sit staring at my three-year-old vows, running my fingers through my hair, straightening it, letting it go, feeling it curl up tight against my head.

"You think with your hair," Tyler'd laughed at me just the other day, when we were working on our creative writing magazine, *Connections*, trying to figure out which illustration would go best with one of Blake's poems.

No matter how many times I run my fingers through my hair tonight, my brain stays muddled. Not about the drug part. I've seen enough of how drugs mess people up to last me a lifetime. I'll never break that promise. The sex part, though? Is that old promise something I should forget about, like Tyler says?

I *want* to stay a virgin. No way could I handle having a baby yet. And no way could I handle an abortion. Or HIV, or herpes, or genital warts, or any of that stuff we hear about in health ed. No way! I do *not* want to go there. I'm sure Tyler doesn't have any diseases 'cause he's never been with anyone else. But that's what Amber thought about her boyfriend, too, and then — herpes. And even if I don't worry about STD with Tyler, there *is* the pregnancy thing. Nothing is absolutely safe except abstinence. That's what I know.

I stare again at my old journal entry. My handwriting is round and slanted backwards. That was back when I was still trying to write like Amber.

I reread the entry, reread my promise to myself, and I know for certain the decision I made back then is still right for me. But the other thing I know for certain is I really, truly, with all my heart, want Tyler to be happy with me.

CHAPTER

5

I decide to write about finding the baby on the trail for the autobiography assignment. *That* experience changed my whole perspective on life.

I start, *"You don't know me unless you know about the baby on the trail."*

As I write, the events come back to me, like it was yesterday instead of four years ago.

This one day my grams and I had sandwiches, apples and drinks in our backpacks, along with the rolled-up faded picnic blanket she'd had since she and my grampa were first married. We were on our way up to Clark's Peak, where there's a waterfall, and picnic tables. It had rained the night before and no one else was around, like we liked it.

We came around a bend, just before the spot where we'd seen a rattlesnake the year before. I was leading the way and I always was a little more careful along this part of the trail, after the rattlesnake incident, so I was moving slowly. There was a noise, maybe real, maybe my imagination. I stopped cold.

"Listen," I whispered.

"I don't hear anything," Grams said.

"Shhh. Just listen."

We stood still and quiet for what seemed like a long time, and then I heard it again, a kind of mewing sound.

"Maybe a kitten."

"I don't think so," Grams said, and started walking carefully toward the sound.

She very gently poked around in the low bushes, searching.

"Careful," I said, remembering rattlers and rodents that bite.

I leaned in beside her, watching her scrape dirt away from a mound just under the closest bush. There was that weak, mewing sound again.

"My God! My God!" she said in something between a whisper and a prayer.

"What is it?"

I got close and peered down, not understanding at first what I was seeing.

"Lauren, get the blanket out of my pack, and open a water bottle for me. Quick!" she said.

She was on her hands and knees, digging around the dirt-covered form and then she carefully lifted it out, supporting its back and head. It stirred, choking, mewing, and I saw that it was not an animal, but a baby. A dirt-caked, blood-caked, human baby. Grams poured water on the edge of the blanket and started cleaning dirt and gunk from the baby's mouth.

"Quick! Give me your sweatshirt and go call 911 from the car!"

She paused just long enough in her cleaning job to pull her car keys from her pocket and toss them to me.

I've never run so fast in my whole life as I did that day. Over rocks and muddy places, up rises, down the hill. I didn't even slow down when I came to the parked car — just banged into it and opened the door in one quick move. At first I couldn't get the phone to work. I dialed 911 over and over and nothing happened. Then I figured the phone battery was dead, but it might work if

I started the car. I was only thirteen, so I sure didn't know how to drive. I had to do *something* though. The nearest house where I might use a phone was at least a mile away.

I slid behind the driver's seat, put the key in the ignition and turned, pressed the gas pedal, and it started right up. Then I dialed again and this time it worked. I told the dispatcher where we were and how to find us, then turned off the engine and ran back up the hill with all the speed and energy I could manage.

When I got back the baby was wrapped in my sweatshirt and Grams had her whole mouth over the baby's, breathing into it, feeling its chest rise, letting the air come out and then breathing into it again. I'd never seen a brand new baby before, but I was pretty sure the bluish color of its face was not a good sign. It sputtered and Grams pulled back. We watched as it took irregular, gasping breaths.

Grams gently rubbed its head and arms, crooning to it that it was going to be okay, everything was going to be all right. I wasn't so sure, but Grams sounded as if she believed it.

It seemed like hours, but it was really only a few minutes, when we heard the siren in the distance, getting louder and louder.

"Go meet them," Grams said, and again I took off. About half way down the trail I saw them running up, lugging equipment. I turned and ran back, with them following right behind me, to the spot where Grams and the baby were.

Then everything started happening — they used a suction thing to be sure there was a clear air passage and then there was an oxygen hookup and a heart monitor and someone talking on a two-way radio giving the baby's vital signs and passing on instructions. I noticed as they let my sweatshirt fall away and placed a soft clean blanket over the baby that it was a girl. I don't know why, but right then I wanted to cry. Maybe I was thinking about what a hard time it was for me, when I was born, and wondering why some kids have to have such hard times. For sure the little baby on the trail didn't deserve to be dumped and left, like a piece of worthless garbage.

Off to the side one of the paramedics was talking with Grams and taking notes. She, the paramedic, motioned to me to come over.

"Tell me exactly what happened, from your perspective," she said.

So I did. Just the way I'm telling you right now. Except I left out the part about how sad it made me.

Pretty soon the paramedics had the baby secured on a small stretcher and were hurrying with it down the hill. Grams and I followed them to the hospital and we were treated like next of kin, with nurses coming out to report on the baby's condition.

Someone, a doctor, or nurse, or paramedic, started calling the little baby Hope, and the name stuck. The newspaper said "Hope" was a perfect name for the trail baby, because as long as there are people in the world like me and my grams, there's hope for the future. Without us, or someone like us, the baby would have had no hope. For a while my grams and I were treated like heroes. Really, it was Grams that saved the baby, but she always reminds me that I was the one who heard it. The mayor honored us both at an annual luncheon of local people who'd done important things. We each got trophies and also our names are engraved on a plaque that is displayed in a glass case at City Hall. The Red Cross also honored Grams because her basic knowledge of first aid had made the difference between life and death for Baby Hope.

But here's the thing that really, really, shocked me. It turned out that Baby Hope was the daughter of Sarah Mabry, who was this super popular girl at Hamilton High. She'd been Homecoming Queen, and was even pregnant *then*, and nobody knew, not her boyfriend, or her mom, or anyone. When she started having contractions, about three weeks after Homecoming, she drove to the foothills, walked halfway to Clark's Peak, gave birth to the baby all by herself, and dumped it under a bush along the trail.

When the police started trying to figure stuff out, they found the afterbirth a little farther down. Really, they found it because of all the turkey vultures flying around and swooping down. Yuck! It makes me sick to think of it.

About a week after we found the baby, the police had pretty much figured out whose it was. Sarah confessed and had to go to court — there was a picture of her in the paper, head down, hands over her face, right next to the picture of her as Homecoming Queen. Right then, even though I didn't know Sarah, I knew her life was ruined. And I promised I would never do anything to let myself get in such a mess.

It is after two in the morning when I finish the "Baby on the Trail" draft. This is the one I'll turn in to Harper — not the rotten mother druggie story. It's easier to think about the baby on the trail — to think about Hope.

I've told a lot in this draft, but I haven't told everything. I haven't told how ever since that day, if I'm worried and confused about my life, I go back to that exact place on the trail. I think about Baby Hope, and how her desperate mother left her there to die. Usually I take my journal and write, sitting by Hope's bush. Being there, writing, helps me figure out how to do what's right.

I *could* tell about that in my autobiography, but so far I've kept my visits to Hope's place a secret. Not that people don't walk past it all the time, but it has a special meaning to me. *Tyler* doesn't even know that I go there. Amber doesn't know, either. It's where I helped save a life, and it's sort of a sacred place to me.

No one knows where Baby Hope is living now, or what her new name is, or who adopted her. Sometimes I wish I could see her. I keep track of her birthdays. She's nearly four years old by this time, and whenever I see a four-year-old, I try to figure out what Baby Hope would be like now. I'm glad no one knows where she is, though, because I don't want Hope to know her mother didn't love her.

As much as Grams and Tyler love me, I always know I started out as a reject. I especially remember that I'm a reject when things aren't going well, or someone's mad at me. I know how much that hurts, and how it robs a person of a certain happiness, or security, or something. It's good that Hope will never know she started out as a reject.

Before we turn in the first drafts of our autobiographies, The Harp has us read our opening sentences out loud.

"We're only going to read that one first sentence. No discussion. No judgment."

Tyler's is "You don't know me without you know I'm hungry to taste life."

A perfect first sentence for Tyler. That tasting life business is what keeps him and his mother mad at each other. Tyler wants to bungee jump, and snowboard, and eat sushi, and ride a motorcycle. His mother wants him to be safe and not do anything with the slightest risk. Secretly, I'm on his mother's side. I'm big on safety. But part of what I love about Tyler is his sense of adventure, and how he wants to dive into life. Even with plants — he wants to know everything about them, and experiment with new ways of planting, and feeding, and pruning — stuff even my gardening grams doesn't think about doing.

Blake's first sentence is, "I *bet* you don't know me — don't know the depths of my soul or the height of my fantasy."

Kelsey's is, "You don't know me because I hide from you."

All of the first sentences are interesting. Some are surprising. But if there were a prize given for most shocking, it would go to Shawna. She is the last to read her sentence.

"You don't know me without you know my father is a royal *asshole!*"

It's as if the whole class stops breathing, waiting for what's next. The Harp is cool. He keeps the same noncommittal expression he's worn for all the other first sentences. Then he collects the papers.

For the rest of the period, we work in groups. Tyler and I, along with Megan, Kelsey and Blake, are in the group that's supposed to be getting ads for the *Connections* publication. It won't come out until May, but there's a whole lot to be done before then. Most of us in the class are seniors, and we want this to be the best magazine ever.

"We should try that new karate place, over near the park," Blake says. "A high school magazine would be a perfect place for them to advertise."

"Do you know anyone there?" Tyler asks.

Blake shakes his head. "Do I look like I hang out with the karate crowd?"

Kelsey says, "No way, Blake. You're too fat for karate."

Blake laughs, but I wonder if his feelings are hurt. That's Kelsey though, all talk, no thought.

"Well, you want to give them a try?" Tyler asks, ignoring Kelsey's remark.

"Sure."

Tyler adds "Karate Studio" to the list of places to contact, and writes Blake's name beside it.

"How'd you do with Chic Boutique, Kelsey?"

"Fine. Like it?" she says, standing and indicating her new sweater set and matching skirt.

"He means did you get the ad, Airhead," Megan says with a laugh.

Kelsey sits down. "Not yet, but soon. The assistant manager just has to convince the manager."

We spend the rest of the time deciding who's going to try to sell ads at which places, and arguing about whether it's better to go in with someone, or alone.

"Alone seems more professional," Tyler says.

"Yeah, but we're *not* professional. We're kids," Megan whines.

"What do *you* think, Virgo Lauren?" Blake asks.

I throw my pencil at him. "You never forget anything, do you?"

"You don't know me without knowing I'm a Capricorny with a big moon rising," he says.

That gets us all laughing. I don't know why. It's not really that funny, but Blake is funny, just the way he says things. And Tyler has a cute kind of snorty laugh, and that always gets the rest of us laughing, too.

Harper scoots a chair into our circle and sits down. He watches for a moment, indulging us, then asks, "How many ads have you sold?"

Tyler hands him the page. Harper glances at it, hands it back.

"Well, it's early yet. Don't forget to hit up your relatives, even down to the third cousins, once removed."

"What's *that* mean?" Kelsey says.

"It means ask everyone in the world to buy an ad," Megan tells her.

"Right," Harper says. "We can't print this baby without money. No lucre, no literature."

"Lucre?" Kelsey says.

"Money," Megan says. "You should be paying me to interpret."

"Well, how'm *I* supposed to know what *lucre* means? I never took Spanish, you know," Kelsey says, all indignant.

Harper laughs a kind of sad laugh, then says, "Maybe you *will* be in my novel after all, Kelsey."

"Cool," she says.

"Don't forget those business card ads. They don't look as good as the larger ones, but at least they're something. Also, try asking them, if they don't want to place an ad, would they like to make a donation."

Harper moves on to the next table and we list more ideas for ad sales.

The last ten minutes of the period are for group reports — how the cover contest is coming along, what arrangements can we make with the school print shop, who's doing word processing and proofreading — the business of putting it all together. That's how it goes in here on Mondays and Wednesdays. On Tuesdays and Thursdays we read submissions, short stories, poetry, essays. We rate each piece in a secret ballot. Then we discuss it. Then we rate it again. Everything is submitted anonymously, to keep the voting based on merit rather than popularity.

On Fridays we take turns reading our own work and making comments. No matter what else we do though, everyday, everyday, everyday, we write for fifteen minutes. "Writing calisthenics," Harper calls it. "Torture," Kelsey calls it. But I'm used to writing.

I started writing a sort of diary way back when I was seven years old. I'd have probably started earlier, but I didn't know how to write that many words until I was seven.

After school, Tyler and I, and Blake, go down to Barb 'n Edie's to try to sell an ad for *Connections*. Barb 'n Edie's is this kind of dumpy place which has been a hangout for Hamilton High kids since the first time bell-bottoms were in style. It doesn't look like much, but the garbageburgers and the onion rings are about the best in the world.

"I hope Edie's in today," Blake says.

"I agree. If Barb's there I think we should leave and come back when we can catch Edie."

"Barb's okay," Tyler says. "You just have to understand her."

That's how Tyler is — he thinks everyone is okay if you just can understand them. I love him for that, along with a lot of other things.

"You talk to her then," Blake says.

"No problem," Tyler says.

When we open the door Barb is at the counter and Edie is nowhere to be seen.

"She's all yours, Tyler," Blake says.

"First we have to buy something," Tyler says, leading us toward an empty booth in the back. "Principles of basic salesmanship. First have a business transaction on the potential buyer's own territory, then they're more likely to later do business with you on *your* terms."

"I can hardly wait to sell an ad to the Acura dealership. Which model do you think we should buy?" Blake says, all sarcastic.

"Very funny, Blake," Tyler says. "But you'll see. What'll it be? French fries? Onion rings?"

We decide on onion rings and sodas and Tyler goes to the counter to order. I watch him talking with Barb. Her frown turns to a smile, then I hear her laughing. Tyler has this way with people that makes everyone like him.

"What was wrong with your friend, Amber, the other day?" Blake asks.

"Oh, just girl stuff."

"I like to know about girl stuff," Blake says.

"Well, you'll have to ask Amber if you want to know about *her* girl stuff 'cause what she told *me* was confidential. Why are you so interested, anyway?"

"I love her from afar," Blake says.

I laugh, but he doesn't and I get this strange feeling that he may not be kidding.

"She's off men," I tell him.

"But the fire still burns," he says, quoting from some poem.

Tyler comes back juggling onion rings, sodas, and a filled-in ad form. He puts the food on the table and waves the ad form in front of us.

"Half page, top price plus an added $10 donation!"

"You da man!" Blake says, high fiving Tyler.

"You da man next!" Tyler says.

"Or, you da woman next," Tyler says, high-fiving me. "You're always the woman," he says more softly, putting his hand under my hair and rubbing my neck, warming me.

"You're always the man," I tell him, taking his hand and holding it against my cheek.

"Gimme a break! Give it a rest!" Blake begs.

"Jealous?" Tyler asks.

"No, just having a reaction to the sugar overload."

We all laugh, then turn our serious attention to the onion rings.

Our next stop is Century Books and Stationery. We agree that I'll take this one, because I buy books here sometimes. "Then you can take the pet store, Blake, 'cause of your big puppy eyes," Tyler laughs.

"No, because I like to pet," Blake says with a leer.

"Don't be juvenile," I tell him.

Inside the bookstore I ask the guy at the cash register if I can see the manager. He points in the direction of a small office in the corner of the fiction department. "Mr. Swallow," he says.

Blake and Tyler thumb through magazines while I go back to the office and knock on the door. I get all shaky when I have to talk to strangers, *especially* if I'm trying to sell something. But I keep telling myself it's important for us all to do our part — I have to do my part. I knock on the door and hear a gruff, breathy voice say, "Enter."

I push open the door and it's like I've stepped back in time. A fat old man with low-riding reading glasses is sitting at a heavy wooden desk with an old-fashioned green shaded lamp. There is no computer, and the telephone is black with one of those rotary dial things.

I take a deep breath and remember to introduce myself, the way we practiced role-playing in class.

"I'm Lauren Bailey," I say, extending my hand toward the old man. He doesn't reach out to shake hands with me, and I'm not sure what to *do* with my hand now that it seems to be hanging out there in the air. We didn't role-play that part. Slowly, I bring my hand back to my side.

"I'm a student at Hamilton High and every year we publish a collection of student art and writing. Would you be interested in advertising . . . "

He doesn't let me finish the sentence and when I try to hand him an information sheet, with prices and ad layout examples on it, he won't even look at it.

"I donated money to the choir tour last year and no one bothered to send me a thank-you note," he says.

I think he must have emphysema or something, because he keeps coughing little coughs, and taking short, fast breaths.

"We're a different group," I say.

"Ingrates. No manners."

"This is a literary . . . "

Again, he cuts me off. "I'm busy," he says, making a sweeping motion with his hands, as if to sweep me out the door.

"I buy books here," I tell him, in a desperate attempt to get through to him.

"You don't *look* like a reader," he wheezes, again doing the sweeping thing. "I'm busy now," he says.

I leave, slamming the door behind me. My face is hot with anger and my heart is beating hard and fast. I march over to where Blake and Tyler stand talking. When they see me they stop.

"Wow," Blake says. "I guess *that* went well."

"Very funny," I say, turning and walking toward the door. They catch up to me.

"What happened?" Tyler asks.

"He wouldn't listen to *anything*! I even told him I buy books in his store but that didn't help, either."

"So much for the buy something theory," Blake says.

"It worked at Barb 'n Edie's," Tyler fires back.

I keep ranting. "Mr. Swallow, the old *bird*, is mad because *choir* didn't send him a thank-you note last year and besides he's a sexist, racist bigot. He said I don't *look* like I'm a reader!"

Wild with anger, I take a book off a counter display and throw it, hard, down on the floor. It makes a loud bang. Everyone in the store is looking at me. Let them look. I reach for another book.

"Hey, hey. It's not worth it," Tyler says, holding both my hands in his. "Calm down," he whispers. "It's okay. Take slow, deep breaths."

I take a deep breath, then another. I see Blake looking at me strangely. I'm so embarrassed. It's like something gets hold of me sometimes and I hardly even know what I'm doing. We walk slowly out of the store and stand in front, on the sidewalk.

"Okay?" Tyler asks.

"Yes," I say, leaning my head into his chest, trying not to cry. After watching awkwardly for a few moments, Blake says, "I'll walk on to the pet store."

"See you there," Tyler says.

Blake walks away and I stay close to Tyler, my hands trembling.

"You shouldn't let things get to you like that," Tyler says.

"I know. I just get so angry sometimes."

"I'm telling you, you should read that book, *Don't Sweat the Small Stuff.*"

"I don't feel much like joking right now."

"I'm not joking," Tyler says, giving me a long look.

We catch up to Blake just outside Paula's Pets. He goes to the counter and asks for Paula.

"Hey, Paula!" the guy at the cash register bellows out.

"Yo!" yells Paula from the back where she's unloading cases of cat food.

Paula's about five feet nine and I bet she weighs at least three hundred pounds. She's got tattoos on both arms, and they're not those pretty henna things that fade, either. One's an eagle and the other's an anchor. She's got arms like Popeye the Sailor Man.

Blake goes back to make his sales pitch and Tyler and I wander around the pet store. There're some really cute black and white puppies in a cage filled with cedar chips. I can't help laughing as I watch them tumbling all over one another.

"Better now?" Tyler asks.

"Thanks," I say, thinking how lucky I am that Tyler's there for me.

After we watch the puppies play, we go to the back of the store, where there's an aquarium filled with iridescent fish. Sitting on a perch above the aquarium is a trite parrot that keeps squawking "Polly wanna cracker? Polly wanna cracker?" We wander down an aisle and stop to watch two tortoises in a giant glass cage. The label on the front identifies the male as Tommy and the female as Teresa. One of them is trying to mount the other. The mountee, Teresa, I suppose, keeps walking away, like she's not even noticing, and the mounter, Tommy, is totally determined to climb up and hang on. I didn't know they did it that way. Truthfully though, I never gave much thought to the mating habits of tortoises until just this instant.

Tyler pulls me close to him and whispers, "Have you thought about what I've asked you to think about?"

"You're *soooo* transparent," I say, smiling up at him.

"I'm *soooo* serious," he says.

Tommy finally has Teresa cornered and is on top of her, apparently doing his thing.

"Come on, we shouldn't be watching their private moment," Tyler says, leading me back to the wholesome little puppies.

"Teresa doesn't seem very enthused."

"Tommy's a brute. You've got to admit, I'm much more sensitive than a tortoise," Tyler says.

Blake comes walking past us, flashing a subtle thumbs up. We follow him out the door.

"Full page ad!" he says, waving the completed form in front of us. "*Now* who's da man?"

"You da man!" Tyler and I shout in unison.

"Way to go, Blake," Tyler says.

I get quiet, thinking what a blob I am that I couldn't even sell a business card ad and Tyler and Blake have both made big sales. It's like Tyler knows what I'm thinking.

"You'll get lucky next time," he says.

He takes a a few strands of my hair and pulls gently, three times, meaning "I love you."

That brings me out of the dumps. I give Tyler's wrist three quick pinches, meaning "Love you, too."

"I can't wait to show *this* to The Harp," Blake says. "He said I'd never get a dime out of Paula. I guess he doesn't know *everything*. Cool, huh?"

Blake waves the paper in front of us again, doing a silly kind of dance, and we laugh, again. The thing with Blake is, most of the time he acts like nothing matters and then he gets all excited, like a little kid, over selling an ad. As my grams would say, go figure.

6

Late in the evening, as I'm dozing over my math homework, Grams calls me to the phone.

"It's Tyler," she says. "Tell him I want him to look at my Japanese maple the next time he's over. The leaves are developing a brownish tip and . . ."

I hand the phone back to Grams.

"Skip the middle person," I say.

"Listen, Tyler," she says, launching into a detailed description of the leaves on her Japanese maple.

"What do you think? Not enough water? Too much?"

She listens for a bit, then thanks him and hands the phone back to me.

"He's a genius," she says. "Tell him I said so."

I take the phone back to my room and close the door.

"Grams says you're a genius."

Tyler laughs the snorty laugh that makes me laugh, too.

"I hope the stuff I recommended doesn't kill her tree."

We start on one of those slow, sluggish conversations that happen after you've been with someone most of the day and don't have anything new to say.

"What're you doing?" Tyler asks.

"Homework. What're you doing?"

"Homework."

"What homework?"

"Chemistry. What about you?"

Even though our talk starts out kind of boring, we always want to talk to each other every night. We ask each other obvious questions and give obvious answers. Then Tyler says, "Blake told me he saw you and Amber at Carole's Coffee yesterday."

"Yeah. I cut English with her. She was really upset."

"Why?"

"Amber doesn't want me to tell anyone."

"I tell *you* everything," Tyler says.

"Well . . . You have to promise not to tell a soul."

"I promise."

"Absolutely no one, not Blake, not even the roses in your garden."

"I promise!"

"Amber has herpes."

There's a long silence, then, "That sucks. Poor Amber. I always thought she was a virgin, though. She seems the type."

"Whatever that means," I say.

"Well, you know. Like, she's not *with* anyone is she?"

"She had a boyfriend that she was all in love with. They did it *once* and then about two weeks later she got a bunch of ugly symptoms. He hadn't even told her. He said *he* was a virgin, too."

"So does she have to take antibiotics or something?"

"There's no cure. That's why she's so freaked out."

"Damn," he says, and again there is a long silence.

"You know for sure you don't have to worry about anything like that with me," he says. "Right?"

"Right," I say. "But that's exactly what Amber thought, too."

"What do you mean by that?"

"Well, you know. She thought he'd never had sex before. She

thought he couldn't possibly have a disease like that. And he'd promised to take care of her and be careful and all, but when the time came he didn't even have a condom. And she was so innocent, she was too embarrassed to even *ask* about a condom."

"But *I'm* not like that!"

"I didn't say you were."

"No, but you're acting like it!"

"I'm not either! I'm just telling you. You asked me to tell you and I'm telling you and now you're getting all mad!"

"I'm not mad! But why don't you trust me?"

"I *do* trust you!"

I hear Tyler breathing deep breaths, like maybe he's trying to calm down, using the same method he always tells me to use. Finally he says, "Listen. Believe me. I don't have any diseases. The whole world knows I'm a virgin. Ask *anyone!*"

"It's not that . . . "

"I'll use a condom. I'll get foam for *you* to use. Just trust me."

"I do. You know I trust you."

"Well, then?"

"Well then, what?"

"Well, then, what about making this weekend our special time?"

Now it's my turn to take slow, deep breaths.

"Well?"

"Can't we just . . . you know . . . keep doing what we've been doing?"

There's another long silence. Then Tyler says, "I don't think that's enough for me anymore. I don't want to pressure you, I'm just telling you how I feel."

"I'm not sure . . . "

"But if you loved me . . . "

"Oh, Tyler. I do. I love you more than anything, it's just . . ."

"Whatever," he sighs, and hangs up.

I dial him back, but all I get is his answering machine. I want to tell him how much I love him, but that's not something I can leave on the machine, for his whole family to hear.

I try to concentrate on math, but all I think of is Tyler — what he wants to do, and what I'm not ready to do. I mean, we do almost everything else. We help each other — you know — reach a climax. But just safe sex ways. That's what we agreed on when we first started getting close. I told Tyler I'd decided a long time ago that I wouldn't have sex — the *total* sex thing, until I was married. He thought that was fine at the time. He even said he respected me for it. But now he's changed. He wants it all.

I close my math book. I don't care. What will I ever need that stuff for? I want to be a writer, not a mathematician.

I keep thinking of Tyler, his smile, his laugh, how secure and warm I feel with his arms around me. I *do* love him. He knows that. Why do I have to prove it to him by breaking my promise? Is that loving *me*? But honestly, I want it, too. I want that special closeness with him. Why is life so confusing?

There's a knock on the door, jarring me out of my thoughts.

"Finished with the phone, Lauren?" Grams asks.

"Oh, yeah. Sorry," I say, passing the phone to her.

"I need to make a quick call to Betty, then I'm done for the night. You going to bed soon?"

"Probably," I say.

"You seem worried. Anything wrong?"

I swear my gramma has some kind of ESP.

"I guess I'm just tired," I tell her.

"Well, if you need to talk, remember I've got a good ear."

"Thanks," I say, forcing a smile and trying to look happy.

It's true my grams is a good listener, but I'd rather not discuss the details of my sex life with her.

"Get a good night's sleep. Things usually look better in the daylight."

I turn my lamp off and stare into the darkness, listening to the gentle hooting of the owl. I've run my hands through my hair about a billion times and my thoughts still aren't clear. What if I said yes, and the condom broke, or had a leak in it? And what if the foam wasn't effective? That stuff happens. And what if I got pregnant? No way could Tyler and I support a baby, or take care of it. And I'm not sure I could handle having an abortion. I don't ever, ever, want to be so stressed that I'd even *think* of doing anything as awful as Sarah Mabry did.

I want to be totally, absolutely, undoubtedly safe from pregnancy. But I want Tyler to be totally, absolutely, undoubtedly happy with me, and to know that I totally, absolutely, undoubtedly love him, and if breaking my old promise is what it takes, well . . .

In my heart I know I've got to reach a decision, but right now my head is spinning with yes-no-yes-no-yes-no.

Before zero period I wait for Tyler at our usual place, on the bench by the tall, scrawny palm tree near the student parking lot. I'm eager to see him, to feel his light morning kiss and to walk, holding hands, along the cracked and gum-studded cement walkway that leads to Hamilton's main campus. Our night-time phone conversation and the sound of Tyler's last, distant "whatever" floats through my head, and I want it to be wiped out by his cheerful "Hey, Curly," greeting.

I wait until after the tardy bell, then walk slowly to class, looking behind me so often I feel stupid, each time knowing I'll see him running up behind me, smiling, breathless, explaining that his dad stopped for gas on the way to school, and Parker cried because he was going to be late, so his dad went out of his way to drop Parker off first. But it's all my imagination. He's not there. No matter how often I look, or how hard I wish, he's not there. And he doesn't show up for creative writing, either.

In peer communications I pretend to be listening but I can only worry about Tyler. Is he really mad at me? Will he stop loving me? The thought leaves me feeling strange and empty.

Ms. Woods hands out photocopied lists of all the topics we put on the board yesterday, and tells us we'll need to choose a subject for our class project.

I look down at the list, but the words blur together. Nothing makes sense. I raise my hand and ask to use the restroom. Woodsie hands me the big, blue hall pass and I walk quickly down the corridor, across the food court to the C building, then upstairs to room 201. I open the back door, just a crack, and see that Tyler is sitting over by the window, where he always sits. The teacher glances up, but I quickly close the door and rush down the stairs.

Even though I hurry back to class, I know I've been gone longer than the usual restroom break. Ms. Woods gives me a look when I return the hall pass to her desk, but she doesn't question me.

When I sit down, Amber passes a note back to me.

"Number Two?" it says.

"Number Zero," I write, and pass the note back.

"I feel better today," she writes back.

I draw a big smiling face at the bottom of the paper and hand it to her.

"Lauren, are you bored with class discussion?" Ms. Woods asks.

I shake my head no.

"Then perhaps you could pay attention?"

I nod yes, feeling all embarrassed.

"Amber?"

"Sorry," Amber says.

"So, tomorrow we're going to have a panel of recovering drug abusers. They'll give some factual information, share some of their personal experiences, and answer questions. I want you each to write out two questions that somehow relate to drugs, and have them ready for the speakers," Woodsie says, handing a stack of 3 x 5 cards to the first person in each row. "Take a card and pass it back," she says.

"Do we hand these cards in, or what?" Scott asks.

"Put your name on one side, in the middle, big print. On the other side write your questions. Keep them until after the discussion, then I'll collect them."

"Can we ask *anything*?"

"What did you have in mind, Scott?" Woodsie asks.

Scott turns red.

"Well?" Woodsie stands waiting.

"Well, like . . . someone told me once, like . . . well . . . "

"Just say it!" Mark says, pounding his desk.

"Sex is better with coke but worse with heroin," Scott blurts out.

Mark laughs a sudden loud laugh, but it's more of a mean laugh than a happy laugh.

"Is that true?" Scott asks Woodsie.

"*I* wouldn't know, Scott, but someone on the panel may. We're trying to encourage open communication here, and if you think the question is appropriate, ask it."

Mark laughs again, then pokes Scott and tells him in this mock whisper, "I hear coke gives you a really big dong!"

The whole class gets quiet, watching Woodsie.

"Stick around for a few minutes after class, will you Mark?" she says.

"Hey! Open communication! Are you another big hypocrite or what?" He bangs his desk again, open palmed, so it makes a loud, slapping noise.

"Just stick around," Woodsie says. "Any other questions about tomorrow?"

"Are they talking about *kids* doing drugs, or *parents* doing drugs?" Shawna asks, holding up her list of subjects.

"I can't say for sure," Woodsie says. "There'll be five of them." If it's at all like the last time they were here, there was an age range from about nineteen to forty-something and they talked about all kinds of drug-related issues."

"I'm sick of always hearing about how awful *kids* are when

parents get away with some really bad shit!"

"Stick around for a few minutes after class, will you Shawna," Mark says, mimicking Ms. Woods. Ms. Woods makes eye contact with Mark, giving him a look that says she's had enough. He looks down at his desk.

"Shawna, work out your questions in a way that addresses the issue of parents doing drugs. I'm sure our panelists will answer as honestly as they can."

Mark mutters, "Yeah, *I* have to stay after but when Doggie Shawna talks bad, no problem."

He says it so softly, I'm not sure anyone else has heard. I glance at Shawna, but her face is hidden by her hair.

7

On the way to English, after peer communications, Amber says, "That skater guy always seems mad at the world. Shawna does, too."

"You should hear Shawna's first sentence for her autobiography," I tell her, immediately wishing I hadn't.

We've all promised that whatever goes on in creative writing is confidential to that group. Otherwise, people might be afraid to write honestly.

"What is it?" Amber says.

I hesitate, not wanting to break a confidence.

"Come on! Spit it out," Amber says, nudging me lightly on the arm.

"Well, what you said about Shawna being mad at the world?"

"Yeah?"

"She's way mad at her father."

"Is that all?"

"That's all I'm saying."

"They're both freaks."

"I don't know about Mark," I say. "But Tyler says you just

have to understand Shawna. He says she's nice, once you get to know her."

"Maybe. Remember, in sixth grade she was like everybody else — quiet, but not obviously strange? Then, in the seventh grade she started with that hair down over her face thing, and wearing those massive, heavy flannel shirts over huge jeans, winter *and* summer."

"Yeah," I say. "I guess I'd forgotten how she used to seem normal."

"Now, though, no kidding, I can easily imagine her picture under one of those newspaper headlines, '**Loner student kills fourteen with grandfather's automatic rifle.**'"

"I'm glad your sense of drama has returned," I say.

"What would your Tyler say about *that* I wonder — if his nursery partner went ballistic?"

I turn away, not wanting to show my sadness, not wanting to think that maybe he's not *my* Tyler anymore.

Amber keeps looking my way until I finally have to turn back toward her.

"Hey, what's up?" she asks.

"Nothing," I say.

"Whoa. I spilled the beans to you the other day. Whatever it is can't be as embarrassing to talk about as the big H problem."

"It's just . . . "

"Not Tyler? You guys are the perfect poster kids for young love."

"I think he's mad at me."

By this time we're at the door to our English class.

"You want to go for coffee and talk?" Amber asks.

"We better not," I say, knowing I'm on the verge of a **D** in English, anyway.

"Turnabout's fair," Amber says. "It might help to talk. It helped me."

"Snyder'd kill us if we cut his class again," I say, walking into the classroom.

Schools are so schizoid sometimes. Yesterday Mr. Snyder was all mad at us because we cut Monday. He wouldn't let us into class until we had a readmit slip. So that meant we had to go to the attendance office, where the line was like waiting for Space Mountain at Disneyland. So it took all period to get that stupid piece of paper stamped readmit. So not only did we miss Monday, we missed yesterday, too. I don't much care, but does it make sense? He's mad because we missed a day, so he makes us miss another day?

I sit at my assigned desk and Amber sits across from me.

"What's Tyler mad about, anyway?"

"I don't even know for sure he's mad. But he sounded mad last night, when we hung up from talking on the phone, and then he wasn't at the bench this morning. But he may not even be mad. I hope he's not mad."

"Okay, okay," Amber says, sounding irritated. "*If* he's mad, what's he mad about?"

"It's kind of private."

"Like herpes isn't?" Amber whispers. "I spilled my guts to *you*, so out with it."

"Sex. He wants sex," I whisper.

"Intercourse? Penetration? The whole package?"

She can be way too loud at the worst possible times!

"Don't broadcast it!"

"Oops, sorry," she whispers.

She looks around to be sure no one's paying attention, then leans in close to me.

"Don't do it! You'll be sorry!" she says.

"Maybe it's not that simple," I tell her.

"It *is*! Look at *me*. The same thing could happen to you!"

"Tyler's not like Keith was."

"Yeah, I didn't think *Keith* was like Keith was, either, but he was."

"Huh? Could you repeat that please?"

"Oh, you know what I mean!"

"I've known Tyler a lot longer than you knew Keith," I remind her.

"So? You don't know everything about him. He could have been with someone else and not wanted to tell you, afraid he'd hurt you, or you'd get mad. Guys are like that, they don't bother to tell you important stuff if it might *inconvenience* them."

"You sound bitter," I tell her.

"Yeah, well I've got a right to be bitter. You'd be bitter too if you spent much time with itchy, oozy sores all over your private area."

"Yuck!"

"I'm just telling you," Amber says, looking all intent. "Don't let any guy talk you into anything you don't want to do."

"But, I love him so much," I tell her.

"Yeah, well, true love waits. If he loves you he'll understand."

"I hope so," I say.

Mr. Snyder has given us two full days of silent reading and independent work in class, so those of us who are behind in the *Jane Eyre* assignments can get caught up. I think it's partly for him to get caught up, too.

He has a huge stack of papers spread out on his desk, and his grade book open in front of him. He's nice enough and knows his subject, but he strikes me as one of those teachers who's marking each day off toward retirement, like a prisoner might mark off days left in his sentence.

I'm reading *Angela's Ashes* tucked inside *Jane Eyre*. Snyder's always preaching to us that we've got to have a background in the classics or we'll never be truly educated. But right now all I want to do is read about Frank McCourt. Maybe it's that I know McCourt's story is true, and *Jane Eyre* is made up.

One thing I know about Frank McCourt is, he read whatever he could get his hands on, classics or not, and he hasn't said a word about *Jane Eyre*. I think even Mr. Snyder would have to agree that McCourt is educated. Anyway, that's my excuse for being sneaky and reading *Angela's Ashes*.

I'm reading the part about how Frank thinks his father is like the Holy Trinity, with three people in him, the nice one in the morning who reads the paper and drinks tea with him, and the other nice one at night, with stories and prayers, and the bad one who smells of whiskey and drinks up all their money.

I don't get that trinity stuff. How can a person be three things at once? Maybe God can do that — but just a plain old person? I don't think so. To me, Frank's dad undid everything good when he drank up their food money, and their rent money. To me, the dad was a murderer, letting his children go without the things his drinking money could have bought, letting them die of complications of not enough food, or warmth, or medicine. He was so awful, he didn't deserve to be alive. Like Marcia. Like Sarah Mabry.

Just at the part in the book where the family gets a letter from the dad saying he'll be home for Christmas and everything will be different, I sense someone standing over me. I don't want to look up because I know it's Mr. Snyder.

"Miss Bailey?"

He reaches down and takes *Angela's Ashes* from where it rests in the novel I'm *supposed* to be reading.

Shaking *Angela's Ashes* in his bony, dark-spotted hand, Mr. Snyder says, "I assume this means you've finished *Jane Eyre* and are ready for the test right now?"

I shake my head no.

"Where are you in *Jane Eyre*?" He frowns down at me. "Be honest."

"Where she's in trouble," I say.

"My dear, that could be anywhere in the whole book. Might you be more specific?"

"Umm, she's at that school," I say, flipping frantically through the pages of the book.

"Find your place, then bring the book up to my desk and we'll talk about it."

Finally I figure out where I am — page 68, where this Mr. Brocklehurst guy is making Jane stand on a stool while he tells everyone in the whole school that Jane is a liar. I check the assignment sheet in my notebook. I'm *supposed* to be on page 249. Oh, well . . .

I take my book up to Mr. Snyder's desk and show him the page I'm on.

"Please, have a seat, Miss Bailey," he says, indicating the chair beside his desk. I know he's really mad because he's being so formal.

"Now, tell me, Miss Bailey, if you can. Is this a remedial class? Or is this an honors class?"

"Honors."

"And is it not an *honor* to be in this class?"

I nod, though right now I'm not exactly feeling honored.

"Well, then. By Monday morning you must be caught up with your reading, or we'll consider a change of classes."

"But . . . "

"No. I warned you about not keeping up last week, and the week before. No buts this time."

I sit, waiting, while Mr. Snyder shuffles papers on his desk.

"That's all. See if you can get some reading done before the end of this period."

"Could I have *Angela's Ashes* back?" I ask, standing.

"Ummm. Monday morning," he says.

"That's not fair," I say.

"Nor is it fair for you to lag behind in your assignments."

I stomp back to my desk and slam *Jane Eyre* down with a loud bang.

"Miss Bailey?"

"It's not even *legal* for a teacher to take a student's own book away from them!"

"Oh? Hire a lawyer then," Snyder says, turning his attention away from me to Scott, who has asked a question about the symbolism of some storm in the novel.

I want my book back! I'm so angry I want to scream and throw things. Instead I sit down at my desk and take deep breaths, like Tyler always tells me to do, and I try not to sweat the small stuff. It doesn't seem like small stuff, though.

I open *Jane Eyre* and stare at a page. Amber gives me one of those shame on you signs she learned from her old-fashioned mother, one index finger scraping across the other, pointed in my direction. Everyone is watching. In my head I hear Grams' voice saying what she always says when I get really mad — Don't let your anger get the best of you. That always makes me wonder, what is the best of me anyway?

When Amber and I leave English, I start ranting about Snyder.

"What right does he have to take my library book? And what does *he* care what I read during independent time anyway? There's got to be some rule against taking a student's property."

Amber looks at me thoughtfully. "Now it's *your* face I can see under the shooting headline instead of Shawna's," she says.

"Oh, yeah, right. 'Student drowns fourteen with grandmother's high-powered water pistol.'"

"There'd be a picture of you, proudly holding a squirt gun, wearing camouflage," Amber laughs.

"And water-wings," I manage to croak out.

It's not really that funny, but Amber and I crack up over it

We lean against the wall, laughing ourselves silly. It's dumb, but at least for a little while I forget my problems.

We're still leaning against the wall, wiping tears of laughter from our faces, when I see Tyler coming my way.

As soon as I see his grin, I know things will be fine.

"See ya," Amber says, walking off toward her third period class.

"Sorry I missed you this morning," Tyler says. "My mom and I got in this big argument about Nana staying at *our* house and taking care of me and Parker there, instead of Parker going to

Nana's."

Tyler shakes his head in a sign of disgust. "She really ticks me off. I'm old enough to pay for my own clothes, but I still need Nana to babysit me? Give me a break!"

"So is your nana coming over on the weekend?"

I don't know what answer to hope for. In a way it would mean less sex-pressure for me if Ms. Hughes *were* coming over. In another way it would be a big disappointment because it's great to be with Tyler when there's no one else around.

"I finally convinced her I was a big boy," Tyler says. "But it took a long time to do it."

He gives my hand that little "I love you" squeeze and for the moment all my old virginity promises are forgotten. Luckily we're in the middle of a school hallway — not exactly the appropriate setting in which to lose one's virginity.

"My mom . . . "

"She's trying to do what's right for you, Ty. Think of it that way."

He smiles. "I know. You're right. I'm lucky to have a mom that cares."

"Really," I say, wondering what it would be like to have a mom that cares. That's something *I'll* never know.

"I can hardly wait for Friday," Tyler says, grinning his glorious grin.

8

This is a minimum day, no volleyball practice, so I'm home by one in the afternoon.

"Grams?" I yell as I open the back door.

"In here," she says. "The living room."

She is stretched out on the couch. Her face is all puffy — like she's been crying.

"Grams? What's wrong?"

She shakes her head and looks away. "It's nothing," she sighs. "Just the day."

"The day? What's wrong with the day?" I ask, then suddenly remember. October 6. The day Marcia died in the explosion.

My grandmother is one of the original positive thinkers. Almost nothing gets her down. If it's broken, she fixes it. If she can't fix it, she goes on to the next thing. But October sixth is always a bad day for her. And Christmas, too, sort of.

"I'll never figure out what went wrong," she says. "I wasn't a perfect mother, I know that, but . . . "

She sighs, looking at the faded family picture that still sits on the mantle. Everybody looks happy there, like a TV family.

Marcia is fourteen in the picture, and Aunt Claudia is sixteen.
Grams still has brown hair and my grandfather definitely doesn't
look like a man with only five years left to live.

"I just can't help thinking about her today. My precious
daughter." She looks away, but I know she's crying. "She was the
happiest child and then . . . "

I stand, helpless, not knowing what to say. Then I say what's
in my heart.

"She threw her life away! She got me born addicted. I *know*
the reason math is so hard for me is because she messed up my
brain before I was even born. And she treated you like dirt."

"Still . . . "

"I hate her." I say.

Grams is quiet for a long time. Then she tells me she used to
be very angry with Marcia, too. But she had to get over it to get
on with her life. I nod my head, as if I understand. But the truth
is, I don't want to get over it. I hate Marcia and she deserves it.
If she'd loved me, I wouldn't hate her. But she didn't even love
her own daughter.

"It was the drugs," Grams says. "If she'd stayed away from
the drugs . . . Oh, I suppose I made plenty of mistakes. Maybe I
didn't notice until it was too late that things had gone wrong. I
didn't want to believe my own dear daughter could be in such
trouble . . . "

It's really hard for me to see Grams so sad. I hug her and go
back to my room. After staring at the bird feeders and watching
the squirrel scare birds away, I decide I need a change of scene.
I tell Grams that I'm going to Amber's for a while. It's just an
excuse. Amber's not even allowed to have friends over except on
weekends. To keep from being a total liar, I drive to Amber's
house. I stop "for a while," like I told Grams I was going to do.
But instead of going in I sit in the car at the curb, blocked from
view of anyone at Amber's by the big hedge in front of her house.

After Amber's, I drive up Garfield, following it all the way to
where it ends at the edge of the foothills. I park and start up the

trail toward Clark's Peak. After only about fifteen minutes of walking, I turn and look out over the valley. On some days I can see all the way to the ocean from here, even to the island that sits alone, twenty-six miles from shore. Today, though, I can't even see the steeple on the big church just a few short miles away. The smog blankets the valley, gray and dense and heavy. It's one of those days where it's best for our health if we don't breathe.

I continue up the trail to the spot where we found Baby Hope. I take my backpack off, get my journal out of it and then sit on the pack. I start writing, anything that comes to my mind — the smell of sage brush, the sounds of rustling leaves, the heavy gray air, the filth of the world, Tyler. Tyler. Real sex or pretend sex. Grams' sadness. Incomplete sentences. Incomplete thoughts. Marcia, blown to bits twelve years ago. Her own doing.

What was it like to give birth to a baby right here, on this trail, so early in the morning the sun wasn't up yet? What an airhead prom queen trick that was! Poor Baby Hope. Her first taste of life in the world was being left alone, cold, no one to care for her. Damn Sarah Mabry! Damn Marcia Bailey!

We found her, though. We saved her. I soak up the sense of Hope that surrounds this special place. I think of good people — Grams, Tyler, Amber, Blake, Mr. Harper. I think of Hope out there somewhere, being loved and growing strong. I'll bet she's smart. I'll bet she can already print her name.

Life is better now. Better than it was before I came up here. At least that's how it seems to me. I write a bit more in my journal, then pack up and walk back down the trail.

I go to the library to see if they have another copy of *Angela's Ashes*. No luck. I browse around there for a bit, then go to the McDonald's drive-thru and get hamburgers and soda, then take them to the nursery.

"Hey, Curly. Nice surprise," he says, glancing at the clock. "Just in time for my break, too."

We sit on two upside-down pots, eating and talking. When

Tyler goes back to work I go home. It is after eight when I get there. Grams is sitting in her big, purple, overstuffed chair, her legs pulled up underneath her, like a kid. She doesn't look so sad now.

"Feeling better?" I ask.

She points to Stephen King's name emblazoned across the front of a book about as thick as my *College Dictionary*. "I needed something to take my mind off things. But now I'm afraid this guy's going to keep me awake and on edge for the next week . . . Want some hot chocolate?" she asks.

I hesitate for a moment. What I really want right now is to be alone with my thoughts. But then I remember how sad Grams looked when I left. I can't turn her down.

"Hot chocolate would be cool," I say.

At first she looks puzzled, then laughs. "Cool — hot chocolate coming up."

I watch her mix powdered chocolate into a pan of nonfat milk and stir it over the burner 'til it gets tiny sizzle bubbles in it. I get a whiff of the chocolate aroma and the scent reminds me of a long ago time when I was five, and I sat in my grandma's kitchen feeling lost and scared.

"I'm sorry I was such a grump today," Grams says. "It's so predictable — I should simply go hide in a cave every October 6, but I always think this time will be different. And it's the same, year after year. I remember what a sweet baby your mother was, and her laugh. I remember how she stopped eating meat when she was in the sixth grade, because she didn't want any animals to be killed for *her* food. She worried so much about your grandpa's lungs that he finally quit smoking. Over and over I ask myself, how did it happen? How could someone like my Marcia have turned into such a . . . a lost soul."

She turns away from me and I see her shoulders tense with the effort to hold back sobs.

I go to her and put my arms around her. She shakes her head. "Oh, I'm not fit company for anyone on this day. Your mother gave me the greatest gift in the world when she had you. That's what's important for me to remember."

We stand in the kitchen, hugging, for a moment. I feel my gramma catch her breath, still trying not to cry.

"I hate that she still makes you so sad, and that she didn't take care of me, and that she got me on drugs before I was born. She was a rotten mother and I *hate* her."

"She's to be pitied."

"Why? She didn't pity me. She let my head get full of lice and she didn't feed me right. She let me be born addicted and probably damaged at least the math part of my brain."

Grams sighs, picks up the wooden spoon and gives the chocolate milk mixture one more stir. She pours a cup of chocolate for each of us.

"Let's talk," she says, carrying the steaming cups out to the living room. I follow. Grams takes her place in the purple chair and I sit on the floor in front of the coffee table.

"You have every right to be angry, to hate your mother. Over time, though, the anger and hatred will hurt you more than anything she ever did to you."

"I can't help it," I tell her.

"Lauren, I know you have a loving heart. The creator of the universe gives us all loving hearts. But when love turns to anger and hate, it's like a cancer in your soul. Don't let that be you."

"It's under control," I tell her.

"I'm not so sure," she says. "Sometimes your anger seems to get the best of you."

"I'm never sure what you mean when you say that," I tell her.

"Remember that time last month, when old Mr. Miles came banging on our door to complain that I parked my car in front of his house too often?"

"That was so *stupid* though," I say, embarrassed at the memory of that day.

"Of course it was stupid. But your reaction, yelling and threatening to shove him off the porch, was a bit over the top."

"But I didn't touch him."

"But you were angry out of proportion to the situation. That's all I'm saying, Lauren. It's just something for you to think about," she says, leaning forward and running her hand lightly over my head.

I think about how angry I was with Mr. Swallow. I think about how Blake looked at me when I threw the book on the floor, like I was some kind of weirdo, and how Tyler keeps telling me not to sweat the small stuff.

We sit quietly for a while, then Grams tells me some things I've not heard before.

"I don't like to dwell on the past. What's done is done and it's our job to make the best of our lives in the present. But your mother was a delightful child. And your grampa, Ray, was crazy about her. He was crazy about Claudia, too, but Claudia was always a little more reserved. Marcia would crawl up on Ray's lap and tell him she loved him . . . she had him wrapped around her little finger. But then, sometime around fifteen or sixteen, things changed. Her grades dropped. We started getting calls from the attendance office that she wasn't in school. She became secretive. Once she put a padlock on her door. Ray went berserk — went to the hardware store and bought a lock cutter. He not only took the lock off the door, he took the door off its hinges."

I look back at the picture over the mantle, trying to imagine the scene with those people.

"That was the first time she ran away," Grams says. "We filed a missing person's report. Then Ray drove to all of her friends' houses, trying to find her. The trouble was, the ones *he* knew weren't her friends any more. They'd been friends from Girl Scouts, and soccer, and the days before Marcia was lost to us. After two weeks, the police found her and brought her home. She'd lost weight. She was filthy and her hair was so dirty it hung together in clumps. Ray took one look at her and walked back to our bedroom. He lay on the bed and sobbed.

"Marcia yelled that she hated it here — hated us. That she'd just run away again, and she did. We both did all we knew to do to try to get her back, but the Marcia we knew was gone."

"Was she using drugs then?" I ask.

"I'm sure she was. We didn't think so at the time — didn't want to think so. But looking back on it, I can't imagine what else would have brought such changes. Later, though, in all those letters from prison, she sounded like the old Marcia. You can't read those letters without feeling her love for you, Lauren."

"Yes, I *can*," I say. "They're fantasy. She didn't do one loving thing for me when she got out of prison. She took me away from a safe place with you, to live in some drug lab."

"She wasn't all bad, though. It's best if you can see that. Will you at least try? Try to let go of some of the anger?"

I nod my head, though I'm not sure I *can* let go of the anger. And besides, if I did, it might ruin my volleyball game.

CHAPTER

The day the ex-druggies come to peer communications I sit way in the back of the room instead of up front in my usual place near Amber. I don't even want to go to class, but I can't afford another cut. Really, though, why should I listen to stuff I already know? What are they going to say? Drugs messed me up. Don't do drugs. Etc. Etc. Puhleeze. I already know all that stuff, and I already know I'll never do drugs.

I sit in the back, where I can work on the second draft of my "Baby on the Trail" composition for creative writing and not be noticed. Except Shawna notices. I swear she's reading over my shoulder — every word I write. It makes me nervous. I dig out the 3 x 5 card with my druggie questions on it, then close my notebook. I'm trying *not* to pay attention when Woodsie asks me to read one of my questions.

"Address it to someone on the panel," she says.

Since I wasn't listening when they introduced themselves I sit there with a blank look on my face.

"Ask Helen," Shawna says, nudging me.

"Who?" I whisper.

"Helen. The fat one," she says, too loud.

I can tell Woodsie is losing patience. I call on Helen, since that's the only name I know.

"Helen, why did you start doing drugs?"

"Well, as your friend there so *kindly* pointed out, I have a weight problem — always have had. When I was in high school I started on cigarettes and amphetamines so I could lose weight. I know most of you don't think of cigarettes as drugs, but they are."

"Did it help?" Mark asked.

"If you mean did I lose weight, I sure did. But I wouldn't say it helped. I'm twenty-eight years old and I look about forty. I've got heart problems, and no one in my family even speaks to me anymore."

"That's cold," Scott says.

"Unless you consider that I stole from them, even the antique coins my father's grandfather had given him."

"You stole from your own family?"

"Yeah, well, I needed a hit. And it was easier stealing from *them* than from strangers, 'cause I knew where to find everything of value."

I swear, these people disgust me so much! Why can't we have a panel of people who're working on a cure for cancer, or even who do beautification projects — something worthwhile, that's what I'd like to hear about.

I check out the panel more carefully now. Next to Helen there's this Latina with big hair and lots of make-up. I don't know how old she is, but she's not young. Next to her is a white guy, with a ring in his eyebrow. He looks like he weighs about ninety-five pounds. On the end is a black guy in a white shirt and tie, looking like the president of a bank or something.

I open my notebook again and try to concentrate on the "Baby on the Trail" story. Why should I care if Shawna's reading it? We saved the baby. *We* were making things better instead of worse. Not like a bunch of irresponsible, thieving drug addicts.

I'm hearing the drone of classroom discussion, not listening to the words, trying to find a better way to describe the stretcher the paramedics used for the baby, when Shawna nudges me and I hear Woodsie call my name. From her tone, I think she's called me more than once.

"Lauren?"

I look up. "Yes?"

"Lauren, is it asking too much for you to pay attention?"

I *want* to tell her yes it *is* too much to ask, but instead I just say, "Sorry."

"Do you have another question?"

I do have a question. It's not one of the ones I've written down, but it's something I used to think about a lot.

"Why do people who are on drugs have babies?"

"I'll take that question," the black guy sitting on the end says. "Lauren? Is it Lauren?"

"Yes."

He looks at me for too long, dark eyes boring into me, like he can see inside my skull. I look away.

"Lauren, people on drugs aren't planning anything but the next hit. So they can feel good. So they won't feel miserable. And when they're feeling good, they may feel good enough to have sex. But they're still, in the back of their mind, planning for the next hit. Where can I get it? Where can I get the money for it? Maybe they're having sex not because they're feeling good, but because someone is paying them for it. So they can *get* the next hit. And they're not thinking about pregnancy, or AIDS, or anything else. When people are on drugs, they're subhuman. I was subhuman for a long time. I'm working hard to be human again."

It's real quiet in the room when the business-type guy is talking. When he stops, I glance up. Our eyes meet. Again, I look away.

"Subhumans should be in the zoo!" Shawna says, her voice filled with anger.

"Possibly," is all he says.

Mark starts laughing his head off. Woodsie walks back to where we're sitting and stands by his desk. He puts his head down on the desk to stifle his laughter.

"Anyone in here who's never made a mistake?" the skinny white guy asks. "I made a mistake. One simple mistake. And it's costing me my life. I've got full-blown AIDS, and none of the new stuff works for me. I keep getting sicker and sicker, no matter what combination of medication they try."

There's a long silence.

"Maybe there'll be a cure pretty soon," Scott says.

"Look at me, man. Do I look like I've got time to wait for a cure?"

He lifts up his T-shirt, exposing his chest. It's got dark red splotches all over it, and he's so skinny his rib cage is nearly as visible as the one on the skeleton in biology.

"All of you, watch out for stupid mistakes. You don't want to end up like me."

The bell rings and I hurry out of the room.

"Intense!" Amber says, catching up to me in the hall. "It's like that AIDS guy is the voice of doom."

"You've been listening to too much of your mom's the-end-is-at-hand talk."

"Maybe it is. You don't know."

"I know people have been expecting the end forever and it hasn't happened yet."

"Well, it's going to happen for Steven," Amber says, all serious.

"Steven?"

"The guy with AIDS who gave us that warning."

"The guy who seemed creepy to me was the black guy who said he'd been subhuman."

"Jacob," Amber says.

"Whatever his name is, I don't know. He kept looking at me."

"I think he was looking at everyone," Amber says.

"Maybe, but it felt like he was looking at *me* all the time."

"I felt really sorry for Angelica," Amber says.

"Which one was she?"

"You know. The one who had her kids taken away from her and doesn't even know where they are?"

"The one with all the make-up?"

Amber stops walking and gives me a long look.

"Were you in the same class I was?"

"Not really."

"What's going on with you, anyway? I thought everything was okay with you and Tyler."

"It's not that."

"Well?"

"Well — I've got better things to do with my time than listen to a bunch of druggies. That guy was right, they *are* subhuman."

"But Lauren! They've all quit! And they're trying to do good things now, like keeping kids from making the same mistakes *they* made."

I feel my fist clenching, the way it does before I serve the volleyball — before I slam my druggie mother in the face. I wish it were volleyball practice time right now, instead of English.

"Lauren?"

"What?"

"You look so . . . strange."

"I'm thinking about my gramma's high-powered water pistol," I tell her. I mean it to be funny, but Amber doesn't laugh.

I guess the herpes crisis is over because Amber shows up to volleyball practice. We give it our best — setting each other up for spikes, or just for fun, always targeting the other side's weak spots, urging each other on.

"S.B.!" I call out, lifting the ball high off my fingertips, over Amber's head.

"S.K.! Back to you!" she calls, as she taps the ball back to me, high.

I jump, my arm reaching way higher than the net. Slam! The Marcia ball that can't be blocked. Amber and I laugh and do the quick handshake that lines up the blood sister spots on our wrists, affirming our blood sister bond.

"That's more like it," Coach Terry says. "See how these two spark the game? Take a lesson from Amber and Lauren. Bring some intensity to the game!"

It's flattering, I guess, but it's mostly embarrassing to have the coach always using us as examples.

After practice we're both starving, so we go to Barb 'n Edie's. Amber sits munching away, first on *her* mountain of onion rings, and then on *mine*.

"Hey, save some for me, will you?"

She looks at her empty plate, then at my plate of mostly eaten onion rings.

"Oops," she says, as if she's surprised.

One thing I know about Amber is that whenever she's feeling tense, she eats everything in sight. I guess she's tense right now, maybe because of the favor I've just asked.

"Could you do this one thing for me?"

"I'm not a liar," Amber says, shoving another batch of onion rings into her mouth.

"I know. But you probably won't even *have* to lie. Just if Grams calls tell her I'm in the shower or something and I'll call her back. Then call me at Tyler's."

Amber looks at me, chewing.

"Look at it this way. I just don't want to worry Grams. She probably won't even call, but if she *does* and you say I'm not there, she'll panic. She'll think I'm dead, or I've turned into my mother, or all kinds of scary stuff."

"Why not tell her the truth?"

"I don't want to get into it with her. If I say I'm spending the weekend with Tyler, she might freak out."

"You think so?"

"I don't *know*. But I don't want to take the chance. Come on,

Amber, this is really, really, really, important to me."

"Why should I help you do something as stupid as losing your virginity?" she says, reaching for the last of the onion rings.

"I *told* you, I'm . . ."

"Yeah, right!" Amber oozes sarcasm. "You're spending the whole weekend, with Tyler, alone in his house, being lovebirds, and you're going to come home a virgin."

Amber's licking her index finger, pressing it down on little pieces of fried batter, licking it again. I sit watching until she notices there's a lull in the conversation.

"What?"

"You can be pretty gross with food sometimes," I tell her, laughing.

"*I'm* gross? I'm not the one planning a big *sex* orgy! That's gross squared to infinity."

"Shhh! It's not a sex orgy and stop showing off with math terms."

I throw my napkin at her and she flicks the last remaining crumb of fried stuff back at me. We laugh until we're gasping.

Finally she says, "Okay, but don't blame me if you get herpes."

"Well, *you're* the only one I know who has it," I say, which sends us into another fit of laughter. I don't know why. It just does.

Amber shows up as planned in the late afternoon. I run out to her car with my backpack and a shopping bag full of clothes for the weekend. Grams stands on the front porch, waving.

"Have fun, you two! See you Sunday."

I wave back, feeling sneaky and guilty.

"Bye, Mrs. Bailey," Amber calls out the window.

We drive to Tyler's and Amber lets me out.

"You've got Tyler's number?"

"Yes. And I still don't like it — your trusting gramma waving at us as if we're off to a Girl Scout weekend instead of me delivering you to an orgy . . . "

"It's not an *orgy*. Stop using that word!"

"Whatever," Amber says. "I've got to get the car back."

I close the door, wave, and take my stuff around back. The extra key is under a pot full of herbs. Tyler won't be home until after ten but that's okay. I told him I'd have pizza fixings ready, and I'm determined to spend at least three hours reading *Jane Eyre*. I figure if I spend three hours each day of the weekend, I'll be caught up by Monday. That should make Mr. Snyder happy.

Between having Woodsie annoyed at me for not paying attention, and Snyder threatening to kick me out of class, and getting **D**'s on my math homework, last week was an academic disaster. Only one month into my senior year and I'm already having to turn over a new leaf.

CHAPTER

10

After an hour with *Jane Eyre*, in which things are beginning to look better for her because she finally has a decent job at a place called Thornfield Hall, I close the book and go into the kitchen to check out the supplies. There's tomato paste and a big can of parmesan cheese and a six pack of soda. I grab my coin purse and walk to the market, about six blocks away. The air is clear and fresh and the San Gabriel mountains look as if you could walk to Mt. Wilson in about half an hour. It's an amazing day for the Los Angeles basin, where the air is usually heavy and gray and leaves a bad taste in your mouth.

As I walk into the market I notice a red Honda Civic parked alone, back by a light pole. It seems like I've noticed it before. But why would I? I'm sure I don't know anyone with a little red Civic like that.

Inside I pick up two ready-made pizza crust things, pepperoni, fresh mushrooms, sliced black olives, and mozzarella cheese. Tyler likes anchovies but, as much as I want to be unselfish, I can't bring myself to buy them. They're so *slimy*.

As I'm turning the corner to Tyler's house I get a glimpse of a red Honda zipping past. There's no reason for me to feel creepy. There must be about a million red Honda Civics running around the San Gabriel Valley. For some reason, though, it gives me an eerie feeling, and I quicken my pace to get to Tyler's. Once inside, I check to be sure all the doors are locked, then I check the windows. As I'm checking the lock on the corner window in the living room, I see a small red car way down at the end of the block. I don't know if it's the one I saw earlier or not. It could be. Or it could all be only my imagination.

After I put the groceries away I pour a soda into an ice-filled glass and take *Jane Eyre* back to Tyler's room. I fluff up his pillows and stretch out on his bed. His room has a pleasant scent — essence of Tyler. I sink into his pillows, happy to be here, and take up where I left off in my reading.

Jane Eyre is secretly in love with this weird guy, Mr. Rochester. It seems as if he loves her, too, but she doesn't know it. As I read, I realize that Jane Eyre and I have some things in common. For one thing, she has no mother or father. And her childhood was awful, living with an aunt and cousins who were so mean to her it's a wonder she lived through it. She didn't have anyone in her life like Grams, either, so she *never* found a safe place, like I did.

Besides being an orphan, and then later being in love, Jane Eyre also expressed herself creatively. She did it with painting, and I do it with writing.

It's easier to pay attention to the book now that I realize that Jane Eyre and I are kind of alike. I'd still *rather* be reading *Angela's Ashes*, but this isn't as bad as it seemed at first.

I'm still reading when I hear Tyler's car turn the corner. It's funny, isn't it, how you can always tell the sound of the car that the person you love drives?

I jump up from the bed and smooth the spread, run brush my teeth, and am waiting on the back porch by the time Tyler parks his car at the end of the driveway.

"Hey, Curly," he says, bouncing up the steps and giving me a big bear hug.

"Hey, Green Jeans," I say, nuzzling my face in his chest.

"I got stuff for pizza," I tell him, leading him into the kitchen. "Are you cleared with your gramma for the weekend?"

"She thinks I'm at Amber's."

"Cool," he says, giving me that meltdown smile of his.

I open the refrigerator and take out the pepperoni and mozzarella cheese, then turn the knob on the oven to start it preheating. Tyler reaches past me and turns the knob to the off position.

I turn it back on.

"The oven's got to preheat," I tell him.

"*I'm* preheated," he says, turning the knob back off. He pulls me close to him and kisses me long and hard.

"I've been thinking of this all afternoon," he says. "Waiting on customers, watering plants, carrying orders to the truck, all afternoon, every step I've been thinking 'Lauren's at my house, waiting for me. Lauren's there.'"

"Don't you want pizza?" I ask.

"There's something else I want more," he says, then kisses me again. His lips are soft and warm. Our tongues tease at each other's lips and I lean into him, feeling the warmth of his body under the roughness of his overalls. He holds me closer, kisses me harder, then takes my hand and leads me to his bedroom.

I get a kind of scared feeling. Ever since our phone call, when we sort of argued about sex, neither of us has brought up the subject. I hope Tyler doesn't think I'm ready to do it *all* just because I'm spending the weekend with him.

Tyler's bedroom is nearly dark, except for the subdued glow of the Mickey Mouse night-light that is always on in the adjoining bathroom. He lies down, crossways, on his bed and gently pulls me down beside him.

"We should talk," I tell him.

"Ummmm, later," he whispers, turning to face me.

He unbuttons my blouse, kissing each newly exposed space as

he does so.

"Tyler, I . . . "

He unbuttons the waist of his overalls and guides my hand inside, to his "friend," as he calls it. Feeling how excited he is gets me even more excited. But we've got to talk. I know we've got to talk.

"Really, Ty . . . "

"Really, yourself," he whispers, undoing my bra and gently caressing my breasts. "You are so amazingly beautiful."

"I don't want to do it," I say.

"Do what? . . . This?" he asks, kissing me lightly on the sensitive part of my neck.

"No. You know," I tell him, breathing fast now. "IT! I don't want to do IT."

He slips his hand inside my pants and finds his way to the wetness between my legs.

"Your body says you want to do it," he whispers.

"But *I* don't," I say.

"Let's just see what happens," he says, moving his hand slowly around my most sensitive parts. "Let's just take all our clothes off . . . We won't do anything you don't want to do, but let's get close. We've never had all our clothes off together."

All of the time he is telling me this he is moving, his hands on me, mouth grazing my skin for punctuation, hips thrusting his friend against my hand, and I'm sinking into the feeling, the sensation, the thrill of Tyler.

He slips my blouse and bra off and I unbutton my jeans. He pulls off his overalls and shirt and tosses them on the floor. He pulls my jeans off and starts to take my underpants off.

"No," I tell him.

He takes his own underwear off then and is totally nude. He rolls over on top of me. We are both breathing strong and heavy, in unison. He tries again to slip my underpants off.

"No," I whisper.

"Please. Please," he says. "I promise I'll stay outside."

"No," I tell him, feeling him strong against me, only the light fabric of my panties between us. I want so much to be as close as I can get, to feel him inside me, I know it would happen if I didn't hold back with that one light barrier.

We kiss, strong. I give him the little bitey kisses he likes around his ears and neck. He moves his hands lower, against my butt, and holds me close to him. He thrusts, easy and slow, rubbing with his "friend" against my secret places, then thrusts harder, faster, until he groans in what sounds like pain but I now know is pleasure. Seconds later, I, too, cry out with pleasure. Our breathing slows, and we lie quiet in the near darkness of the room.

"I love you so much, Lauren," he tells me. "You're all I've ever wanted and I didn't even know it until that day at the nursery."

"I got so scared when I thought you were mad at me. I don't know how I'd go on if you ever stopped loving me," I whisper.

"I won't. I won't ever stop. I just want the whole thing. I'm almost eighteen and I'm still a virgin and I want the whole thing."

"But, aren't you happy right now?"

"Yes," he says. "But I could be happier. I could make you happier."

"I couldn't be happier than right now," I tell him, snuggling even closer.

We doze for a while, then, about midnight, I wake to the sound of the shower in Tyler's bathroom. I turn over and close my eyes, half-remembering a dream of a man and a child, running.

"Awake?"

Tyler is standing over me, a giant bath towel wrapped around him.

"Almost," I say, still trying to see the dream.

"Pizza-time," he says, grinning.

"Now?" I mumble.

"Wakie-wakie," he says, laughing.

He leaves the room and I hear him shuffling around in the

kitchen. I take a quick shower and put on my sweat pants and sweater, then join him. He hands me a soda and I open the tomato paste and spread it over the pizza shell, while he slices the mozzarella into paper-thin pieces.

When the pizza is cooked we put everything on a tray and take it into the family room where they have a TV with a giant screen. We watch "Psycho" while we munch out. At first it's kind of fun, but then that Norman Bates guy is such a creep that I lose my appetite. And then, when the woman's stabbed in the shower — that's got to be one of the scariest things I've ever seen in a movie.

While the movie's rewinding we sit snuggled up, talking about school, and Harper's class.

"I'll be right back," Tyler says, jumping up as if he's just remembered something.

When he comes back he's dressed in his mother's robe, with a blanket wrapped around him, pretending to be Norman Bates.

"Not funny," I say, even though I'm laughing.

"Let me show you to your room," he says.

"Stop!" I say, laughing harder, trying to pull the blanket off him.

A sudden sound at the window makes us both freeze in silence.

"What was *that*?" I whisper, the tingle of adrenalin reaching my fingertips.

Tyler puts a finger to his lips to silence me, then tiptoes to the window and pulls the drape back just a crack. He stands there for a long time, then pulls the drape back farther for a broader view. I walk over to stand beside him.

"Nothing he says — a branch and our Psycho-crazed imaginations."

"Look at that," I whisper, pointing toward the street.

A small car, parked at the end of the block, starts up and drives past the house and around the corner, all with its lights off.

"What about it?" Tyler says.

"Why would they try to sneak by with their lights off?"

"Sneak by?" Tyler grins. "They just forgot to turn them on, that's all."

"No, there's this car that I keep seeing. Sometimes I think someone is following me, and watching me."

"'Psycho' has got you spooked."

"Maybe," I say. But in my heart I know it was that Honda. And I know my spooky feeling is from something more real than a movie.

CHAPTER

Because I've got a game at eight in the morning, and Tyler has to be at work by eight-thirty, we get up earlier than we want to. When I come out to the kitchen, Tyler is pouring us each an orange juice.

"I've got to check my kids before we go," Tyler says, referring to all the stuff he's planted the past few weeks.

I follow him outside and stand watching from the back porch. Tyler looks at each of the new plants and grasses and checks the soil for moisture. He pinches dead flowers off the roses and twines loose morning glory stems around their trellis.

Usually I'm rushing around so much in the mornings I forget to look at things. Standing here, drinking my orange juice, I am caught by the freshness and beauty of the morning. A hummingbird flits around the purple sage, out in Tyler's experimental garden. It all feels peaceful and safe.

Tyler comes back to the porch and sits beside me.

"I've got to talk my mom into letting me dig up the rest of this lawn," he says. "I'll put in more drought-resistant grasses. It's stupid to waste water on a lawn."

"You could probably come dig up Grams' lawn. She was talking about more native plant stuff just the other day. And she's starting a really stinky compost pile."

"You've got the coolest gramma in the world. My nana doesn't know compost from condom . . . Which reminds me . . ."

"No you don't," I laugh. "No more on the subject."

"Yes, more," he says, grabbing me and kissing me, face, chin, neck, hands, kissing, kissing, kissing, saying "More, more, more."

I jump off the porch and run around front, Tyler chasing close behind, laughing.

At the corner of the house I slide to an abrupt stop. Tyler bumps into me, nearly knocking me over.

"There!" I say, pointing down the street, seeing the back end of a red Honda turning onto Cyprus Street.

"What?" Tyler asks.

"The car. The same one that was out there last night . . . It feels ominous," I tell him.

Tyler frowns, thoughtful. "But it could all be coincidence, or imagination," he says.

"It could be," I agree. "It *feels* like something more, though."

We go back inside to get ready for the day, our lighthearted mood now subdued.

"Maybe you shouldn't come back here after your game."

"I planned to read here in the afternoon, like yesterday," I tell him.

"Yeah, but in case there *is* someone watching you, I'm sure there's not, but just to be on the safe side, you shouldn't be here alone."

"I'm not afraid," I tell him, which is not *exactly* true.

"Go read in the library. I'll pick you up there after work."

"I *can't* read in the library. Grams may be substituting for her sick friend."

"And . . . ?"

"And . . . she thinks I'm at Amber's house, working on our

peer communications project."

"Well, I don't want you to be here by yourself. Just the other day I saw on the news how some girl was killed by this whacked-out guy. It happens, you know."

I lean into his chest, thinking how lucky I am that Tyler cares enough to worry about me.

"I feel bad enough about lying to Grams as it is. I sure don't want to run into her in the library and have to make up some other story."

"Well, go read at the mall then. They've got all those tables there. I'll pick you up at the mall, down by the fountain."

"I *hate* the mall. Who can concentrate at the mall?"

"Kelsey," he says with a laugh. "You're the same sign, why don't *you* like the mall?"

He prances around in imitation of Kelsey's hip-swinging sexy walk, getting me laughing so hard I have to run to the bathroom. When I come out Tyler has changed into his work clothes and is leaning up against the kitchen counter, eating a banana.

"Want one?"

"No, thanks."

While he eats, he watches me.

After a minute or so he says, "I know by the way you're pulling at your hair that you're thinking about something. What is it?"

I stop running my fingers through my hair, not even aware I'd been doing that.

"I'm thinking I'll come back here after my game, and read, like I need to do. I'm thinking I'm imagining stuff."

"Yeah. Tonight we'll watch a Disney video."

Tyler pulls me to him and starts giving me short kisses that soon turn into longer ones. Then he stands back.

"*We* can't be doing this! I've got to get to work. You've got a game. What's *wrong* with us?" he says in a fake panic voice, again making me laugh.

I rush into the bedroom and put on my volleyball uniform. I

grab my backpack, with a change of clothes in it. We double check each lock and, instead of putting the extra key back under the herb pot, I put it in my backpack. If anyone *is* watching, I don't want to make the extra key available.

When Tyler drops me off at school he says, "Promise you'll be careful."

"I promise. I'll see you this afternoon."

I give him a quick kiss and sprint over to the gym. Amber is already there, doing her stretches.

"So?" she says.

"So what?"

"So did you do it or not?"

"Do what?" I say.

"You know what I mean! Don't act stupid."

"It's not an act," I tell her.

"Just answer my question."

"If you mean did I lose my virginity, the answer is no."

"Really?"

"Really."

I latch onto a place at the wall, beside Amber, and start stretching my calves.

"What changed your mind?" Amber asks.

"Nothing. My mind just stayed made up . . . I kept thinking about Baby Hope, and Sarah Mabry. How one day Sarah was Homecoming Queen and the next she was almost a murderer. She would have been, too, if Grams and I hadn't found the baby."

"But you wouldn't have to get pregnant," Amber says.

"So now are you going to try to talk me *into* it?"

"No. I'm just saying . . . "

"I know. I've thought about all that stuff, too. Birth control stuff, and stuff that makes getting some STD almost impossible. But it's *all* just almost. *Almost* certain not to get pregnant. *Almost* certain not to get a disease."

"Tell me about it," Amber sighs.

"Besides, Tyler and I . . . I mean, it's not exactly . . . "

"I know," Amber says. "You're one of the 'everything but' girls. I wish I'd been."

"OKAY! EVERYBODY ON THE COURT! CHOP-CHOP!" Coach Terry yells.

We run onto the court for warm-ups and then the Hacienda Hills team arrives. Play starts and I don't think about anything but volleyball. Not sex. Not a little red Honda. Not anything but the game — blocking the net, spiking, banging the serve, return, return, return. Slam the ball. Slam my Marcia. The power of anger. Use the power. Keep it on the court.

Our team celebrates the win at Barb 'n Edie's and then Amber drops me off back at Tyler's. I stretch out on Tyler's bed and take up reading in *Jane Eyre* where I left off yesterday. I love Tyler's room, his things, the scent of him. I know I'm the only girl who has ever been in here and I feel special, knowing I hold an important, one-of-a-kind place in Tyler's life.

When I count pages I see that I can be caught up tomorrow. That's good. I've decided to get things in order so I can maintain decent grades. This first month of school I've been a flake, but now I'm getting serious. If I want to be a journalist I've got plenty of years of school left, so I'd better get with it. It's true I'd still rather be reading *Angela's Ashes*, but *Jane Eyre*'s turning out to be a good story. Already I've copied down a whole bunch of words I want to remember to use in my own writing. Words like "indomitable," and "rapture," "goad," "abhor," and a lot more.

"Don't just live. *Think* about your life. Don't just read. *Think* about what you read." That's what Harper always tells us. Sometimes I don't pay much attention to what teachers have to say, but I listen to Harper because I have so much respect for him. So I'm trying to think about *Jane Eyre*.

One thing I like about Jane Eyre is that she holds to her principles. In a way I'm doing that too, by staying a virgin until I get married.

One big way Jane and I are different is that she loved her dead mother. She even loved the aunt who was so mean to her. She didn't seem to hold any anger toward anyone. *She* probably wouldn't have made a good volleyball player.

I'm reading away, pondering these things, lost in another world, when I hear this loud, peace-shattering yell.

"LAUREN! LAUREN!"

I jump to the floor, my heart pounding.

"What?" I yell, running toward the sound of Tyler's voice. We meet in the hallway.

"Lauren," he says, throwing his arms around me and holding me close. "Are you okay?" He is breathing hard, trembling.

"I'm fine! What's wrong??"

"I saw the car. I saw the man. I thought, what if he'd hurt you? What if he'd killed you?"

Tyler buries his head in my shoulder, slows his breathing, relaxes.

"God. I was so scared," he says.

We sit on the bed and he tells me, "I was coming home from work, maybe a little worried that you were here by yourself, I don't know. And I saw the car, the red Honda, parked down the street. And the guy in the car was peering at my house, not moving, just watching.

"I pulled right up next to him and stopped, so I could get a good look inside his car. Like what if he was kidnapping you or something? He seemed startled, then he quickly started the engine and hurried away. But not before I got a really good look at him."

"What did he look like?"

"He looked mean, and menacing. A big, black guy with evil eyes."

Tyler pauses, shakes his head, then runs the back of his fingers along my cheek.

"I thought you might be dead."

"I didn't see anything, or hear anything," I say.

"You never see or hear anything if you're reading a book."

"I'd have *noticed* if someone was trying to get in, or was prowling around."

"Well, that guy was out there and he was watching *this* house. That big, black guy in his little red Honda."

"Why do you keep saying he's black, like *that's* a big deal?"

"Oh, come on, Lauren. You know the statistics, how many black men are in jail. They had to do *something* to get there."

"I can't believe you're saying this! *I'm* black, you think *I'm* going to end up in jail?"

"Lauren! None of this is the *point.* Some guy is stalking you, and you're going to get mad at *me* because I noticed he's black?"

"No. Just answer my question. Do you think I'm going to end up in jail?"

"I'm worried you're going to end up *dead*! That's what's got me worried . . . Besides, you're not really black. You're not even half black."

"In this country, any fraction of black is black!"

I'm crying now, and I don't even know why, except I can't believe Tyler's attitude and I keep thinking about stalking. Someone might be stalking me.

"Sometimes I don't get you, Lauren. The thing we've got to worry about now is this guy, whatever color he is, who is hanging around, watching you. People don't usually do that with good intentions, you know?"

I lean against Tyler's chest and let the tears come.

"I'm sorry," I say. "I love you . . . I know you're not racist."

I wipe at my eyes, and my runny nose. I'm not pretty when I cry but I can't help it. Tyler holds me tight.

"I was so scared. I love you so much. Oh, Lauren, what if one of us dies before we make love? I mean really make love. The real way."

I sit up straight.

"You were worried I'd die before we had the total sex thing? I can't believe you! Is that all in the world you want from me?"

"You know me better than that, Lauren. God, why do you have to misinterpret everything I say?"

"Why do you have to keep bringing everything back to sex?"

Tyler stomps out of the bedroom into the living room. I hear the TV come on. Why are we mad? I don't even know, exactly. But I feel it, and I feel Tyler's absence from the room. I open *Jane Eyre* again and try to concentrate. After reading a chapter and not being able to remember any of it, I go out to the living room and sit next to Tyler.

"I'm sorry," I say. "I don't want us to be mad at each other."

"I don't, either," he says. "But you put me down so bad. You know sex isn't all I think about. It's a lot, but it's not all."

"But I want you to love me enough that you'll wait — you know, that 'true love waits' thing."

"I know," he sighs.

We sit together for a long time, watching TV, or pretending to watch TV, I'm not sure. I'm thinking about the red Honda again.

"Did you get the license number of the car?" I ask.

Tyler shakes his head.

"I only paid attention to the guy. No way will I forget what he looks like. But I missed the license number — didn't even think about it until the car had turned the corner."

Tyler turns all the living room lights out, goes to the window and peeks through the blinds.

"Nothing out there now," he says.

We get some snacks from the kitchen and settle back in front of the TV. I'm pretty sure neither of us is interested, but it's easier than talking. After a while I go back to the bedroom and read. When Tyler comes in it is late. We sleep side by side, close to each other, but when I try to give him more than a peck, he moves away. In the morning, though, he is cheerful again, and we do what we do, not all that Tyler wants, but what we always do. Then we get up and fix a big batch of bacon and eggs. We take our plates outside and eat on the back steps. Tyler goes once out front to look for the red car, but it's not there.

"We should file a report," he says.

"But I really don't want Grams to know I've been here this weekend."

"Just tell the cops you want it all kept confidential."

"Right. Like that's going to happen. Listen, maybe it was all coincidence. Maybe the guy is new in your neighborhood and had a reason to be there."

"Yeah. And maybe he's the San Gabriel Valley Strangler escaped from prison and up to his old tricks. Remember that guy? Stalk a teenaged girl for a while, learn her patterns, and then find her where he knew she'd be alone and kill her."

"Tyler," I gasp. "That scares me!"

"It scares me, too. You *should* be scared."

CHAPTER

12

*O*ctober 10, 8:30 p.m.
Dear Journal —I love Tyler so much! He ended up telling me he would stop pressuring me about sex. He said if I was sure I wanted to wait until marriage to have intercourse, he'd be satisfied with "outercourse." I am so relieved!

I couldn't stand to lose him over the sex thing, and I couldn't stand to go back on my word —the whole thing was making me crazy.

My grams didn't call Amber's house, so Amber didn't have to lie. I haven't seen the red Honda around for two days. And I'm all caught up with the Jane Eyre reading assignments and Mr. Snyder gave my Angela's Ashes back to me. He even said he read it over the weekend and approved of my outside reading. Everything's so cool right now. —Love, Me

I look back over my journal entry, dig out my list of words from *Jane Eyre*, then work on my writing vocabulary.

Dear Journal,

My love for Tyler is indomitable. He told me he agreed that we should wait to have sexual relations until we're married. All of my worries now are alleviated. I couldn't bear to have him forsake me over the issue of sexual congress. How dreary my world would be without him, yet how I would have abhorred going back on my word —the whole thing was driving me to despair. But now, I am in a rapture of happiness.

All is well with my grandmother. Amber didn't have to tell a falsehood for my sake. The red Honda is gone and my reading goals are accomplished. Happiness and well-being prevail. —

Fondest regards, Me.

Better. Much better. I'm going to keep doing that until I have a vocabulary the size of Webster's dictionary. After all, that's what a writer needs — words. Charlotte Bronte sure had a lot of words when she wrote *Jane Eyre*.

"Lauren?"

Grams is standing at my door, a bunch of pamphlets in her hand. Even though it's my grams' own house, she never comes into my room unless I invite her. Tyler is right, I have the coolest gramma in the world.

"Come on in, Grams," I say, closing my journal.

She leans against the wall, by my desk, and hands me the pamphlets. I glance at what she's given me — information from Planned Parenthood about protection from pregnancy and disease — even a pamphlet about abortion.

"I know I'm old, but I'm not blind," she says. "I know you and Tyler are . . . close."

I leaf through one of the booklets.

"We got all this stuff in health ed," I tell her, not making eye contact.

"It's good for you to have reference material," Grams says. There's a diagram of the proper way to put on a condom. I quick close the pamphlet. My hands are all sweaty. I don't know why. I glance up at Grams. I bet her hands are all sweaty, too. "Look, Lauren, this isn't easy for me. When I was growing up, no adult ever told me about anything. The only words of wisdom related to sex that I got from my mother came the day I married your grampa. Just as she was straightening my wedding veil she got all teary-eyed and told me, 'I only hope he doesn't hurt you too much.'"

"Really?" I say.

She nods. "I'm sure she meant well. And I meant well with your mother and Claudia. I was much more informative than *my* mother had been, but it was difficult for me to be entirely forthright. It seemed almost unnatural to be talking with my daughters about such personal things."

I flip through another of the pamphlets, this time coming to a diagram of the female reproductive system. Grams looks over my shoulder.

"I was nearly forty before I knew the names of all those parts," she says, pointing to the picture.

"We learn that in school," I tell her, turning the page, wishing we could change the subject.

"Well, I want you to be informed," she tells me. "And I want you to know you can come to me with any question . . . "

She pauses, then laughs. "I suppose you know more than I do, anyway," she says.

I laugh, too, but can think of nothing to say.

After a while Grams says, "I don't want to pry into your private life, but I see how important you and Tyler are to each other, and it's only natural to want to express your love sexually, but if you were to get pregnant . . . "

"Grams! I decided a long time ago not to have sex until I'm married. Remember?"

"I remember. But I know a lot can change between fourteen

and seventeen . . . "

Grams gets the look on her face that tells me she's thinking of Marcia.

"I'm not my mother!" I shout.

Grams takes a step back, away from my desk where the pamphlets are spread out.

"Of course you're not," she says, in that calm way she has.

"Just because my mother messed up doesn't mean I'm going to!"

I don't mean to shout, but I know my words are coming out really loud.

"Lauren, please . . . "

Like a fool, I start crying. "I hate how everyone thinks I'll end up like my mother . . . "

"Whatever gave you that idea?" Grams says, coming to me and putting her arms around me.

I sob into her sweatshirt while she holds me close.

"Lauren, try, oh please, try, to see things as they are. Even now you've gone farther in school than your mother ever did. *She* was already addicted by the time she was your age. That's not *you*."

I look up into my grandmother's tender face.

"I'm sorry I yelled at you," I say, catching my breath, trying to stop crying.

Grams sits on the bed. "I didn't mean to insult you by bringing this information to you. I'm not accusing you of anything."

"I know," I say.

"I'm sure this is an old-fashioned view, but in my experience, sex can be a beautiful thing between people who love each other. If there's not love, or mutual respect, it can be ugly as death. I trust you not to get involved in something ugly. And I also expect that you and Tyler are doing more than holding hands."

"Grams . . . "

"Yes, Sweetheart?"

I look away from her. "I'm sorry I lied to you about staying at Amber's when I was really staying at Tyler's."

"You're not a very good liar," Grams says.

"You knew?"

"Let's just say I had a feeling."

"Did you check with Amber's mom or something?"

"You know me better than that. Any worries I have with you are with *you*, not Amber's mom."

I nod my head, feeling small that my Grams is so straight on with me, and that I lied to her.

"Are you mad at me?"

Grams sighs. "I want us always to be honest with each other, Lauren, that's all."

"I won't lie to you again, Grams. I promise."

Grams nods, turns to leave, then changes her mind.

"Lauren?"

I look up at her.

"I've been thinking about the talk we had about your anger, and now, tonight, the business about you thinking that you could turn out like your mother . . . Betty was telling me about a psychologist who was very helpful to her grandson and . . . "

"You think I'm a nut case, don't you?"

"No. But I think life can seem overwhelming at times, and it's good to get help."

"Did *you* ever get *help*?" I say, all sarcastic.

"As a matter of fact, I did."

She gives me a long look, like she's not sure whether or not she wants to say more, then she continues.

"Shortly after your grampa died, I was *so* lonely. Claudia had already moved east, and your mother was lost to drugs. I sat in the house with the blinds closed. For days at a time I wouldn't bother to get out of my bathrobe."

I can hardly believe what I'm hearing from my Grams, who's up at six every morning, bouncing around with energy and enthusiasm.

"Finally Millie sat me down for a long talk, about how there was more to life than feeling sorry for myself, and what would

Ray think if he could see me. So I called my doctor, who recommended a psychologist."

"And you went?"

"I went once a week, for about six months."

"What did he do?"

"She. The psychologist was a woman. She helped me figure out why I was so depressed. *I* thought I was depressed because Ray died so suddenly and I missed him so much. But there was more to it than that."

"Did she do tests on you, or hypnotize you, or what?"

Grams fluffs the pillow on my bed and smooths the spread back over it. She picks at pieces of lint until I wonder if she's going to answer my questions or not. Finally, after what seems like a long time, she continues.

"Dr. Pratt and I just talked, but she knew the right questions to ask — questions I'd avoided asking myself."

"Like what?"

"Like how I felt about your mother, and Claudia, and Ray. She helped me see that depression is a kind of anger turned inward."

"I don't get it."

"I didn't get it at first, either. But once I did, I wasn't burdened with grief or depression any more."

"But . . . ?"

"Unconsciously, I was *very* angry with your mother, for one thing. We'd been the best parents we knew how to be. What went wrong? I'll never understand it. Why would she even experiment with drugs? She *knew* better. She threw her life away for what? A quick thrill? . . . I blamed her for Ray's sudden death. He worried so much about her. She'd been his baby and the thought of her on the streets . . . it was too much for him."

The rage within me boils up! She killed my grandfather! I could have known my grandfather if Marcia hadn't been such a total loser!

"And I was angry with Ray, too, for dying and leaving me alone. If he had loved me enough, he wouldn't have left me."

"But he had a heart attack. Right?"

"Yes. I'm not saying any of this made sense, but it's what I was *feeling.* Dr. Pratt helped me realize that my task had to do with recognizing anger and practicing forgiveness. It sounds easy, but it wasn't."

"But that's all you did with the doctor? Just talk?"

"Talk. And then think about it. And think about it and think about it," Grams says, smiling.

She fluffs the pillow again and again smooths the bedspread over it, as if it needed it. She walks over to where I'm still sitting at my desk and puts her arms around me.

"That's enough of my life story for one sitting. The rest, as they say, is history. I started working at the library, and I slowly started building a new life. A few years later, I found you. You gave me a purpose. That was a great gift . . . Thank you for that."

Grams kisses me on the forehead, tells me good-night, and leaves. I go back to my journal.

October 10, 10 p.m.
Dear Journal, Part II,
  Sometimes I get so confused, and I have these horrible feelings — like everyone thinks I'll end up like Marcia, when almost no one even knows about Marcia. And I feel awful about lying to Grams, and then I get all angry at her which is totally unfair, or I fall apart crying, which I don't understand. And I don't get the thing about how anger is so destructive. It's made me the star player on the volleyball team. Grams is probably right that I need a shrink but what if the shrink finds out I'm in a bigger mess than I think I am? That wouldn't help, would it? —
    Love, Me

Tuesday morning I'm sitting on the old, splintery bench, waiting for Tyler. I'm in such a good mood, first of all that everything's so good with him, and then that I'm totally caught up with my homework, even in math. And I haven't seen the red car for days. It's strange, how upset I was last night, and now everything seems so great. It's probably just hormones or something. I don't think I need a shrink after all.

"Hey!" Tyler yells from way down by the parking lot.

I get up from the bench and walk toward him.

"Missed you last night," he says, giving me a quick kiss on the lips.

"Missed you, too."

"I got used to having you around, night and day, on the weekend."

"Maybe your parents will go to Las Vegas again soon," I say.

"Ummm, Mom lost all her gambling money so they *say* they're staying home for a while."

We walk through half-deserted hallways to creative writing. The Harp isn't there yet so we wait outside with Megan and Zack. Shawna comes up in her usual heavy flannel shirt and oversized jeans.

"Tyler," she says. Not "Hi," or "What's up," or anything like that, just "Tyler."

"Shawna," he says with a grin.

She smiles back at him, this big happy smile, like something I've never seen on her face before. Her eyes are blue-gray. I don't think I'll tell Blake, though. I didn't think so at the time we made the bet, but now, it seems kind of sneaky to be betting on the color of another person's eyes.

The Harp comes sleepwalking down the hall, balancing books, papers and his grungy thermos. We follow him into the classroom where he pours himself a cup of coffee and snoozes in a standing position until the bell rings. Then he snaps awake. The miracle of daily resurrection, Blake calls Harper's morning routine.

After we do our fifteen minute quick-write, Mr. Harper talks a bit about newspaper writing, then tells us about our next assignment.

"You're off to a great start with your autobiographies. I'll get them back with comments the beginning of next week. In the meantime, start thinking about your feature article assignment. This is a writing project that you can work on in groups of two or three. It will require interviews and other means of research and it must deal with a timely topic."

It ends up that Shawna, Tyler and I will work together.

"First off, we need a topic," Tyler says.

Shawna fishes around in her notebook and pulls out the list from peer communications.

"These are all timely," she says.

We go down the list, talking about possibilities.

"How about doing something on AIDS?" Tyler says.

"Too depressing," I say. "How about this right to die stuff?"

"Talk about depressing!" Tyler says. "How about religious cults?"

"Stupid," Shawna mutters.

"How about parents who do drugs?" Tyler says.

"I'm sick of hearing about drug stuff. I don't even want to think about it," I say.

"You don't have to get all mad about it!" Shawna says, not looking up.

"I'm not mad, I'd just like to think about something else now and then," I say, realizing I sound mad. "Why don't we ever think about the good stuff?"

"Well . . . " Tyler runs his finger the rest of the way down the list, then points to the next to last topic.

"How about this? How about Habitat for Humanity?"

"What's that?" Shawna asks.

"You know. Where a bunch of people get together and build a house for a family that needs one."

"I've heard of them," I say. "That's cool."

When The Harp stops at our desks, we tell him we'll do a feature on Habitat for Humanity.

"Good topic," he says. "Where will you start?"

All three of us sit speechless.

Harper walks to the front of the classroom.

"Anybody know anything about Habitat for Humanity?"

"I think some people at our church may be working on a house," Megan says.

"Well, see if you can get a phone number for this group, will you?"

Megan nods.

"That's the same church where Amber and her mom go," I tell Tyler. "I'll bet I can get information from her . . . There's probably stuff on the internet, too."

"What good'll that do?" Shawna says, acting like I've just said something too stupid for words.

"It's a good place to get information," I tell her.

"I suppose *you've* got a big computer at home, with e-mail and internet and all?"

What's *with* her, I wonder?

"I don't have *any* of that stuff at home, but there's always the library. Heard of it?" I ask.

Shawna ducks her head back down and hides her face behind her hair. What just happened? I was in such a great mood less than an hour ago. How did I suddenly become so angry?

"I can tell this is going to be a fun project," I say to Tyler as we walk toward our first period classes.

"It's a good topic," Tyler says.

"Why did *she* have to be in our group, anyway?" I ask.

"I feel sorry for her," Tyler says. "I mean, look at her. What would it be like to be Shawna?"

"She's just so weird."

"She has her reasons," Tyler says.

"Maybe. Anyway, I didn't mean to get mad at her. But she acts like she's never even heard of the internet!"

Tyler looks at me thoughtfully. I wonder if he ever gets tired of my quick mood changes? I'm afraid to ask.

Tyler gives my hand three quick squeezes just as the bell rings.

I squeeze my "love you, too" answer back.

"Later," he says.

I watch, loving him, as he sprints down the hallway and disappears into the sea of students. We've only a few weeks to go before our one-year anniversary. I've been saving my money and I want to get him something special, something that will last.

Everything goes well for the rest of the day. But then, after we're leaving the gym, after volleyball practice, I get a glimpse of the red Honda.

"Look!"

"What?" Amber says.

"That Honda. I keep seeing it, like maybe someone's watching me."

"That's Ms. Woods' car," Amber laughs.

"No! Not the white one! The red one that just drove out the driveway!"

"Oh. I didn't see it," Amber says, leaving me to wonder if *I* really saw it or not.

My imagination? But Tyler saw it the other day. *He* knows the red Honda is real.

"I'll walk home with you if you're scared," Amber offers.

"Oh, that's okay," I say, not able to admit that I'm scared.

I put my hands in my jeans pockets to keep them from trembling, and, once we reach the sidewalk, Amber and I go our separate directions.

13

Thursday after school Tyler, Blake and I go over to the new karate place to try to sell an ad. The guy who runs it, Mr. Raley, asks us to wait until class is over and he'll talk with us. There are about twenty kids, maybe seven or eight years old, in white pajama things with different colored belts. They're constantly yelling "Yes sir," like it's training for the Marines. We watch for about ten minutes while they kick and block and get into unnatural positions. Finally, they say a loud, unison "Yes, *Sir!*" and run off the mat.

Mr. Raley listens while we give our sales pitch.

"I'll buy a full page ad if you get three new people to sign up for a month of lessons."

"Anyone?" Blake asks.

"Anyone from Hamilton High School," Mr. Raley says, then hurries over to start the next class which is already gathered on the mat.

Back in Tyler's car, Blake says, "I bet we can find three people easy."

"I'm not betting," Tyler says.

"I know, I know. You only bet on sure things, like seed identification."

"Maybe Shawna'd like to sign up for karate," Blake says.

"No way. Shawna gives all her money to her mom, just so they have enough for food and rent."

Blake asks the question that's on my mind.

"How do you know?"

"We've been working in the same section of the nursery, repotting plants. It's strange, but Shawna's really different at work than she is at school. At work she likes to talk."

"Does she come out from under her hair at work?" Blake asks.

"Yeah. She talks to Mrs. Shaefer a lot, but sometimes she talks to me, too. Mrs. Shaefer told me Shawna'd had a hard life, but I'm not sure what she meant."

"She helps support her family?" I ask.

"Yeah. Well, her father's in prison. I know that much. Plus she has three younger sisters and her mom has some kind of disease — diabetes I think."

"I'll try to be nicer," I say.

"Me, too," Blake says.

We go through a whole list of possibilities for karate sign-ups. It may not be so easy after all.

"How about your friend Amber?" Blake asks.

Lately it seems that almost every time I see Blake he eventually gets around to asking something about Amber.

"Amber's mother would never let her take karate," I tell him.

"Why not?"

"It's not *ladylike*. Mrs. Brody's got this thing about how Amber's supposed to be *ladylike*."

"What about volleyball?" Tyler says. "That's not exactly something you'd see the Queen of England doing."

"You don't *even* know what Amber had to go through for her mom to let her play volleyball. For every hour on the court, Amber has to read the Bible for an hour. Not just read it either, but outline the major points of what she's read."

"Sounds like child abuse to me," Blake says.

"Amber's used to it. In a way, I think she sort of likes it. She's learned a lot, anyway."

"I'd rather read a seed catalogue," Tyler says.

"Do you think she likes me?" Blake says.

I look at him, puzzled. What kind of "like" does he mean, anyway? Then I see how red his face is getting. I'm trying to picture Amber interested in Blake. It doesn't fit.

"She laughed at something I said once. I think that means she likes me."

"*I* laugh at what you say."

"'Cause *you* like me, too," Blake says.

"No way," I tell him, leaning as far as my seat belt will allow and planting a kiss on Tyler's cheek. "Just one man for me."

"I'm way envious. The two of you have found love, and I'm still lonely and blue, left to love Amber from afar."

It's hard to tell when Blake is being serious and when he's just fooling around, but he may be serious about liking Amber.

"Find out if she thinks I could be the man of her dreams," he says.

"Give it up," I tell him. "Amber's through with men for a while."

"Maybe the while's up," Blake says.

"Just mention Blake's name to her," Tyler says. "See what happens."

"Okay," I say. "But don't expect anything."

"Don't expect anything. Don't expect anything," Blake mocks. "That's what my mom always told me at Christmas time, and then I'd get *everything* I ever asked for."

"I'm *not* your mom."

"What about this? What about if the four of us go to Saturday's football game together. You know, just casual," Tyler says.

"Yeah! yeah!" Blake says, panting from the back seat.

"I think you'd have a better chance with Fiona Walters," I say. Fiona Walters is the most beautiful, conceited girl at Hamilton

High. Even Leonardo Di Caprio wouldn't stand a chance with Fiona.

When we get to Blake's house, just as he's getting out of the car, Tyler says, "I could probably set you up with Shawna."

"Who?" Blake says, as if he can't believe his ears.

I expect to hear Tyler's funny, snorting laugh any second, but he's not kidding.

"Shawna Latham?" Blake says, incredulously.

"Yeah."

"Maybe, but . . . I was hoping for someone I wouldn't have to ask to wear a bag over her head . . . "

So much for being nicer, I think.

Tyler tells Blake, "That's cold. She's a nice person. Maybe if you looked beyond the surface, you *wouldn't* be lonely and loveless."

"Now look who's being cold," Blake says and gets out, slamming the door.

"I hate when people slam my car door," Tyler says as we drive away.

"I can't exactly see Blake and Shawna together," I say.

"Because she's not beautiful, like you?"

"Because she always seems to be in a bad mood."

"Yeah, but you should see her at the nursery, babying plants along and singing to them."

"Singing? Shawna?"

"Yeah. I think Blake might like her if he'd give her a chance."

"I think Amber might like Blake, if *she'd* give *him* a chance. But I don't think she will."

We pull into the driveway at Grams' house. Her car's not there, so I guess she's still substituting at the library.

"You want a soda?"

"Sure."

We go into the house and I get two sodas from the refrigerator. We sit at the kitchen table, talking.

"It's a big deal, being together a year," Tyler says.

"Just a beginning," I say.

He reaches for me. I get out of my chair and stand in front of him. He puts his arms around my waist and pulls me down on his lap. We kiss, a real kiss, not a passing kiss.

"I love you," he says. "Love you, love you, love you."

He runs his fingers lightly across my cheek and along my neck.

"You are so beautiful," he says.

"I love you, Ty," I say, wishing I could say more, find better words, newer words, but that's all I know to say.

He glances at the clock on the wall.

"Can't be late," he says, gently pushing me away and standing up. One more quick kiss and he's out the door.

I flop down in front of the tube and veg out with a blast of MTV. When the phone rings I rush to get it, but when I answer, no one answers back. I call Amber.

"Did you just try to call me?"

"No, but I was thinking about it."

"I don't know why people do that, call and then don't talk."

"Maybe it was the wrong number."

"Probably, but couldn't they just say so?"

"People have no manners these days. That's what my mom says."

Even though Amber complains about her mom a lot, she's always quoting her.

"Listen Amber, if I said Blake McCormack, what would you say?"

"I'd say, 'Who's Blake McCormack?'"

"You know, Tyler's friend, the guy who's always hanging out at Carole's."

"That's half the senior class," Amber says. "What's he look like?"

"Well, he always wears a black baseball cap, backwards. Nice blue eyes, sort of a flat nose."

"Kind of fat?"

"Well, a little chubby, maybe."

"Ratty brown corduroy pants?"

"Well . . . he's going to be a writer. He's supposed to look ratty."

"You're going to be a writer and you don't look ratty."

"I'm going to be a journalist. That's different. Blake's going to be a poet. He's actually named after a famous poet."

Amber groans. "He's strange, that's what I think. Besides, I'm not in the market."

"He's a nice guy, though. And he's funny. You like funny. And he seriously wants a girlfriend."

"What diseases does he have?"

"Come on, Amber. Get over it. You're not going to go the whole rest of your young years without a social life, are you?"

"Without a social life and with a social disease," Amber whispers in the phone.

That gets us laughing. I love that about Amber and me. We can laugh over the worst stuff.

"Tyler suggested he ask Shawna out."

"Shawna, from our class?"

"The same one."

"Let me get this straight. This Blake guy is trying to decide between *me* and *Shawna*?"

"Tyler says she sings to the plants."

"Shawna? I'd have to see it," Amber says. "Maybe *Mark*, from peer communications, and Shawna should get together. That'd be a couple."

"Leaving Blake for *you*."

"I didn't say that."

"Well, think about it anyway. We could go to Saturday's game together. Tyler and me and you and Blake."

We talk for a while about peer communications and Snyder's class, and about the rumor that Arielle Lunden is pregnant.

"That is so *weak*!" I say.

"I heard she wanted to get pregnant."

"That is so *stupid*! How's Arielle going to take care of a baby?"

"Don't know," Amber says. "I'm only telling you what I heard."

"Change subjects," I say.

"Okay."

"I'm trying to figure out what to give Tyler for our anniversary. I want it to be something really special, that he'll always remember."

"Have you got enough money to buy him a leather jacket?"

"Yeah, but I don't think he'd like that. I'd like to give him a little diamond earring, but he refuses to get his ear pierced."

"Give him what he really wants," Amber says.

"Amber! What a thing to say. You're always talking antisex, but then you say something like that. I've *told* you, I'm staying a virgin until marriage."

"Yeah, yeah. I'll bet by the time you're eighteen and a day, Tyler will have persuaded you to break your vow of virginity."

"It's a bet! Tyler's decided that if I want to wait until marriage, that's how it should be."

"Oh, right. I wonder how long *that* will last."

"That's how much he loves me," I tell her. "He doesn't want to do anything that's not right for me."

"Give me a break."

"You wouldn't be so cynical if you let love into your heart," I tell Amber.

"And that would be Blake?"

"Could be."

"Show him to me tomorrow, so I'm sure we're talking about the same person."

"We'll have so much fun! The four of us!"

"I'm not saying I'll go out with him! I can't this Saturday night, anyway."

"Why?"

"Because, my *mom* won't let me go out with anyone unless

they ask at least a week in advance."

"But the door isn't locked, is it?"

"Speaking of doors," Amber says, sidestepping the question. "I've got this information on Habitat houses . . . "

We talk for another hour or so, then I start my homework. Later, Grams comes in with Chinese food and we pig out in front of the news.

I'm back to my homework when the phone rings. I answer, and again it is no one. It gives me a shaky feeling, like something is wrong in my life, and I don't know what it is.

When all of my homework is done, I stretch out on the bed to read from *Angela's Ashes*. Frank McCourt has had a terrible life, with so many people he loves dying, and teachers being mean to him, and his own father deserting him. But he doesn't seem to be bitter or resentful at all. I'd like to ask him how he keeps bitterness and anger out of his heart, but I'm sure he's too famous to talk to me.

I'd like to talk to Charlotte Bronte about *Jane Eyre*, too. Why wasn't Jane Eyre angry and bitter? That's something I'm wondering about more and more these days. Why do I get so angry, when others, who have just as much right to be angry, are mellow and kind?

The phone rings. In a moment Grams is knocking on my door.

"Were you expecting a call?"

"Not especially," I say.

"Surely Tyler's not afraid to ask for you if I answer, even if it is after calling hours."

"It's not Tyler."

"We should have an unlisted number," Grams says. "Next year I won't have them list it."

Grams leaves and I try to go back to my reading, but I can't concentrate. There is probably nothing to be nervous about, but I feel it, anyway.

14

With the help of Amber's mom, we make arrangements to visit a Habitat for Humanity site on Saturday. One of the main organizers has agreed to let us interview her on tape, if we'll help serve lunch.

Amber's decided to join us for the project, to finish up her community service hours. That's a Hamilton High requirement — at least forty hours of community service or no graduation.

Mrs. Brody drops us off around ten in the morning, telling us she'll be back at two to pick us up. Shawna is sitting on the curb waiting for us. Tyler's working today, and Blake's helping his grandmother move, so it's just the three of us.

The house sits on a small lot between two older, slightly rundown houses. It looks like it's almost finished, at least on the outside. Swarms of people are doing stuff, painting trim, putting hardware on windows and doors, working on a porch railing. In the back some guys are mixing concrete, getting ready to pour a slab for a patio.

"Cute place," Amber says. "Not a great neighborhood, though."
Shawna tosses her hair back just long enough to give Amber

a mad look. "I live just around the corner," she says.

"Sorry," Amber says, her face growing red from the neck up.

$\mathbf{A}$ woman dressed in jeans and a flannel shirt walks over to where we're standing.

"Are you the group from Hamilton High?"

"Yes," I say.

"Jackie Salazar," she says, sticking her hand out. "Call me Jackie."

"Lauren Bailey," I say, reaching out and shaking hands.

She's smaller than I am, but what a grip she's got!

Jackie goes through the same routine with Amber and Shawna.

"Come on, I'll show you around, then we can find a spot to talk for a bit."

"Can I start my tape recorder now?" I ask.

"Yeah. I don't know how much you'll pick up in the middle of all this noise, but give it a try if you want."

We follow her inside.

"Today's the day the wallboard goes up," she says, motioning toward a corner where materials are stacked. Two sawhorses are set up in the living room, and two guys are measuring and cutting the wallboard to size. Two women about Grams' age are using nail guns to secure the wallboard in place.

"Every inch of work that's done here is from volunteers. Some know what they're doing, and some don't," she laughs. "It all works out, though."

"Where do you get the money for the materials?" I ask. I'm sort of proud of the question because I know one way for journalists to get a story is to follow the money.

"We get a set amount from national Habitat for Humanity funds, and then we often get donations for extras. For instance, the patio wasn't included in the original plan, but donations of money and labor made that possible. For a family of five, with three kids under seven, the patio will add a lot to their enjoyment of their new home."

Shawna stands with her hands in her jeans pockets, looking at the house, the porch, the yard.

"How do people get one of these houses?" Shawna asks. "My mom and me and my sisters need a house."

"It's complicated," Jackie says. "But I'll be happy to give you an application. The houses all go to families with low income."

"No problem," Shawna says.

Jackie walks over to a worktable that's set up in the dining area, shuffles through some papers, pulls out an application form, and hands it to Shawna.

"Sad to say, but there are hundreds of applicants for each house."

Shawna looks disappointed, but carefully folds the application and puts it in her backpack.

"Does the poorest family get the house?" she asks.

"No, we have a committee. They screen all the applications and evaluate them based on certain criteria."

"Then what?" Amber asks.

"Well, ultimately every application that meets the standards is put into a big container, and we have a public drawing. Whichever application is drawn, that's the family that gets the house. It's very exciting."

"What are the standards?" Amber asks.

"Well, one adult in the family must be working full time. They must have character references from neighbors and previous landlords. No one in the family can have problems with substance abuse . . . "

Shawna reaches into her backpack, pulls out the application and hands it back to Jackie.

"Our apartment's okay," she says, ducking her head so that all we can see is hair.

Jackie pauses for a moment, watching Shawna, then leads us through the bedrooms and baths. Everything is pretty basic. The bedrooms are smaller than the ones at Grams' house. There are two small bathrooms, one with a tub and one with a shower.

There's a nice fireplace in the living room.

The family who's going to live here comes in just before lunch time. The six-year-old boy is in his soccer uniform, jazzed because he'd made a goal.

"It was cooool, Jackie," he says, drawing cool out to make it a three-syllable word.

"I wish I'd been there, Tommy," Jackie says with a smile.

The mom, Mary, is carrying a boy who looks like he's about a year old, and there's a girl about four, maybe Hope's size, clinging to the mom's jeans.

"Where's Richard?" Jackie asks.

"He said to tell you he's sorry not to be here to help pour the patio. He had a chance to work overtime."

"Well, good for him. We've got *plenty* of help here today."

"The extra money'll be enough to buy that bunk bed for the boys' room. He'll come over after work Monday and do some painting to make up for missing today."

"Hey, Mom!" the oldest boy calls from one of the bedrooms.

"Better go see the progress," Jackie tells her with a smile.

Mary and the other two go to the door of the room that Tommy's inspecting.

"Cooool," he says. "Look at these shelves. This is where my hamster cage can go, and here's where Batman and Robin can live, and . . ."

"No hamster!" Mary says.

"But Mom . . . "

Jackie laughs, then leads us into the kitchen.

"These folks are living in a one-room, roach-infested apartment now, upstairs, with no place for the kids to play. You can imagine how thrilled they are to be moving into a three-bedroom place of their own."

Jackie introduces us around to the people working in the kitchen.

"Sam, can you put these three to work?"

"Sure can," he says.

Sam hands us each a big serving spoon and stations us by huge pans set up on a board between the two sawhorses. I serve refried beans, Amber serves rice, and Shawna serves some kind of hamburger casserole. People help themselves to salad, bread, and sodas. After everyone else is served, Amber, Shawna and I help ourselves. We take our plates outside where we find a place to sit on the back steps.

"I'm glad we chose this project. This is cooool," I say, imitating Tommy.

Shawna lifts her head and pushes her hair back away from her face.

"It *is* cool," she says.

"I might like to volunteer some more," Amber says.

Shawna nods. "They'll need landscaping. I could get some plant discards from the nursery — you know, the things that aren't good enough to sell but will grow fine with the right care — I could get a whole bunch of that stuff. Right now there are about ten sick-looking camellias out behind the shed. Nobody wants them. I could teach you how to prepare the soil and all. There's a little orange tree back there, too."

Amber and I both look at Shawna, momentarily speechless. It's the most I've *ever* heard her say at one time, and she's actually smiling.

Finally, Amber says, "Well, yeah. That's a great idea. I'd help."

"I'd help," I tell her. "We could all plant them next Saturday."

"I bet Tyler would help us, too," she says.

"I'm *sure* he would," I say, wondering why I hadn't thought of it first.

We go inside and tell Jackie of our landscaping ideas.

"See, that's what I love about this Habitat for Humanity business. When we start out it looks like we'll only be able to provide the bare necessities, and then things like this just keep happening. That's how we're getting the patio, and how we got the garage, and the fireplace . . ."

"Hey, Mary," Jackie calls to the mom, who is cleaning spackle away from a window in the dining room. "These girls are going to get some plants for us. You like camellias?"

Mary looks at us, smiling broadly. "I am so lucky," she says. "Sometimes I get scared. With so much good, when does the bad come?"

"I keep trying to convince Mary that her balance sheet can take another century of good luck and still not be caught up with the earlier bad luck."

She and Jackie both laugh, but it's more of a wise laugh than a funny laugh.

Mary turns to us. "Thank you," she says. "Camellias are my favorite."

Back in Jackie's "office," she hands us a lot of printed materials about Habitat for Humanity. I'm thinking maybe next week we can come out and take pictures.

At Jackie's suggestion, Shawna, Amber and I interview a few of the other workers. There's a professor of comparative literature, a woman, from Claremont College, who's done the major plumbing work. A guy who works at the Honest Engine car repair place has done most of the electrical work. The two women I noticed earlier who were nailing wallboard have worked every Saturday since the foundation was poured.

When we run out of tape we stop interviewing. It's nearly time for Amber's mom to pick us up, anyway.

"I've got to get back to babysit my little sister," Shawna says.

"You want to wait and get a ride from my mom?"

Shawna smiles. "I live just around the corner, remember?"

Amber laughs. "See you Monday."

"Yeah. I'll talk to my boss about those plants tomorrow . . . Bye." She waves to us, and to Mary who is still working at the front window. Amber and I sit on a pile of bricks by the side of the walkway, waiting for her mom.

"Wow! What a change of personality," Amber says.

"No kidding! It's like she's the grump of the century, and then, once she started talking about the plants she was all transformed."

"I can see why that Blake guy would like her," Amber says.

"He likes *you!*"

"Did you tell him I'm unavailable?"

"He wants your phone number."

"Did you give it to him?"

"*Noooo.* I wouldn't give him your phone number unless I asked you. Can I?"

"I don't know. It would be fun to do something with you and Tyler. But . . . I don't know about this Blake guy."

"It'd be great," I tell her. "We can go to the game next week. If you don't like him you don't ever have to go out with him again."

"Yeah, well. I don't know."

"When I pointed him out to you yesterday you said he was kind of cute."

Amber starts laughing.

"What?"

"I just said that 'cause he was so far away I couldn't even see him."

"Was not!"

"Was too. He was about from here to the end of the block, down where that red car is."

I look quickly in the direction she's pointing.

"That's it! That's the red Honda I've been telling you about."

Amber squints, then stands up.

"I'm going to walk down there and see who it is."

I grab her hand. "No! It's someone weird. I know it is!"

"Well, if it is, they're after you, not me."

She pulls her hand loose and walks away. I'd go after her, but she's right. Whoever it is seems to only be stalking me. I watch as she casually walks down the sidewalk, to the end of the block. I see her come up even with the car, and then the car slowly pulls away. I see her watching and I hope she's noticing the license number. Once the car is out of sight, Amber turns and runs back. I get up and run to meet her.

"Quick. Get me something to write on before I forget. KZY389, KZY389. KZY389," she chants over and over until I can get pencil and paper from my backpack and write it down.

"Get this! I recognized the guy!" she tells me.

"What? Who is it?"

"It's that guy, Jacob."

"Jacob?"

"You know, the ex-druggie who visited peer communications that day. The one that kept looking at you!"

"Are you sure? How can you be sure?"

"I *am* sure. I'd recognize any of those people. I was paying attention, okay?"

"But . . ."

"He was just sitting there. When I stopped and looked in the window though, he turned his head away and drove off. I'm *sure* it was that guy, though."

"But why is he following me around?"

"I don't know. But I don't think people follow people like that, kind of secretly, for good things. Do you?"

"I guess not."

"We should call the cops and give them the license plate number."

"But what am I going to say? I see this car sometimes? They'd think I'm nuts."

"They could at least run a check on the plate, see if the car's stolen, or if it belongs to some recently released sex offender."

"But he hasn't *done* anything."

"Right. It would be good to check him out before he *does* do something, don't you think?"

I mull it over, wondering, too, what the mysterious phone calls are all about.

"Someone keeps calling our house and hanging up when we answer," I tell Amber.

"Maybe wanting to know if you're home," Amber says. "As soon as I get home I'm calling the cops. I don't care what you say. . . . He's a big guy, and he's black, in case you don't remember."

"I can hardly hold *that* against him!"

"I'm only giving you a description, you don't have to get all racially outraged about it."

"I'm not racially outraged! I just don't like it that because he's black he's a bad guy! *I'm* black, remember?"

"It's just a *description*. And anyway, you're only part black."

"That makes me black, and you know it."

"You know what? Sometimes I think you just look for stuff to get mad at. You'd better be getting mad at the guy who's following you around, rather than getting mad at me. I'm on your side, remember?"

"Sorry," I say.

We sit on the bricks, quiet for a while, then we start talking about the pros and cons of calling the cops. As usual, Amber's mom is about twenty minutes late, so we have plenty of time to talk. I pretend to be all calm, but inside my chest, my heart is pounding like crazy.

15

When I tell Grams about the red Honda, she insists on calling her friend, Dennis, who's a sheriff. She tells him the whole story and gives him the license plate number. He says he wants to talk with me in person, and he'll stop by about seven.

"Couldn't we do it tomorrow?" I ask Grams. "Tyler's picking me up at seven to go to the game."

Grams gives me the same look she used to give when I made all kinds of excuses for not making my bed — sort of a "time to grow up now" look.

"This is more important than getting to the game on time," Grams says.

The phone rings and I don't even want to answer it, in case it's another hang-up call. Grams is so used to having me run to the phone that she just sits there, listening to it ring. Finally Grams rushes to the kitchen and answers the call.

"Amber," she says.

"Hey," I say, taking the phone from Grams and walking out to the back deck, ready to settle in for a long conversation.

"He called," Amber says.

"Who?"

"You know. The guy you keep trying to set me up with."

"Blake?"

"Yeah."

"How'd he get your number?"

"He said he found it on the internet."

"But you're unlisted. Can they put your number on the internet if it's unlisted?"

"What're you so worried about my phone number for?"

"I don't know. I'm just, you know, sort of freaked out over all of this business about the red car. My grandmother called the sheriff, and now he's going to come over to talk to me right when it's time for Tyler to get here . . . "

"Don't you even want to know about the phone call?"

That's when I realize what a social misfit I've been, going on and on about my stuff and not even listening to Amber.

"Tell me. What'd he say? What'd *you* say?"

"Well . . . you're right about him being funny. And he was kind of sweet, too. I could tell he was really embarrassed when he asked if I'd go out with him next Saturday. You know, with you and Tyler, to the game."

"What'd you say?"

"Well . . . at first I said no, but then, well, it might be fun."

"YOU SAID YES???" I scream into the phone.

"Yes."

"Wow! Great! We'll have so much fun!"

"Do you think . . . well . . . maybe Tyler could tell him . . . "

"What are you trying to say, S.B.?"

"Do you think maybe he could wear something besides the brown corduroy?" Amber says, practically in a whisper.

"*I'm* not going to suggest that."

"But Tyler?"

"Maybe," I say, but in my heart, I doubt it.

"Tell me about the sheriff."

"Not so fast. Are you going to like Blake?"

"I'm only doing it for you," Amber says with a laugh.

"Right. You're happy about it. I can tell."

"Well . . . I do think maybe it's time for me to stop being such a homebody. I mean, it *is* my senior year and all."

"Yeah, but don't get your heart set on Grad Nite with Blake 'cause I bet he won't be graduating."

"Really? He seems smart enough."

"Oh, he's smart enough, but he's getting his education at Carole's Coffee Shoppe rather than Hamilton High. He sits there most of the day, 'observing,' and writing poetry about what he sees."

Amber groans. "I guess that means he saw me having a nervous breakdown over the herpes flare-up when we were there that day."

"Yeah, he noticed us. But he didn't have any idea what was upsetting you."

"How embarrassing, anyway."

"He's seen lots worse stuff than that in there. You should hear the poem he wrote about this older couple arguing with each other. It shows how mean and degrading people can be."

"His *poem* does?"

"Yeah. You know, it's not like we're doing *nursery* rhymes in creative writing."

"Anyway, I'm tired of talking about Blake. Tell me about the sheriff."

When I'm finally off the phone with Amber, I take a quick shower and put on clean clothes. I dress in school colors — blue and gold. It sounds corny, but it's a tradition at Hamilton High and almost everyone dresses like that for games — even when they come watch our girls' volleyball games. A lot of kids have parents who went to Hamilton High and they wear school colors to games, too. Even some grandparents do. Grams didn't go to Hamilton High, and she's not much for attending games. If we get to the playoffs in volleyball though, she'll come in jeans and a gold sweater. Maybe so many people wear school colors because it's easy. It's not like our colors were ecru and mauve or something hard like that.

On the dot of seven the doorbell rings and it's the sheriff.

"Come in, Dennis," Grams says. "Cup of coffee?"

"No thanks. I don't think this will take long."

We sit across from each other by the fireplace, Grams and me on one sofa and Dennis in the big armchair. He takes out his note pad and starts with the questions.

I describe the car, repeat the license plate number, identify locations where I've seen the car.

"Has the driver ever tried to approach you?"

"No."

"What's the closest you've ever seen the car?"

"Probably about a block away."

"And if you start walking toward the car, what happens?"

"It seems like if the person in the car thinks I've seen him, he drives away."

The phone rings and Grams goes to the kitchen to answer it, then is back immediately.

"Tyler's had to stay late at work," Grams says. "He'll probably not get here until eight or eight-thirty."

"Who's Tyler?" the sheriff asks.

"My boyfriend."

"Oh," Sheriff Dennis says. He rereads his notes, then says, "So there's been no kind of threatening behavior at all?"

"No," I say, realizing how silly the whole thing sounds.

"If I showed you mug shots, would you recognize him?"

"No. But Amber probably would."

"Amber?"

"My friend. She saw him kind of close today. She thinks he was one of the people who came and talked to our peer communications class about drugs."

"Really?" the sheriff says, raising an eyebrow. "What's your teacher's name?"

On and on, detail after detail. Everything repeated twice.

"Any reason this guy would be interested in you?"

"I can't imagine why," I tell him.

Finally, Dennis folds up his notebook and puts it back in his pocket.

"Here's the thing," he says. "I've run a thorough check on the license and the car. Found out the guy is employed by a real estate company. That gives him plenty of reason to be out and about at all times of the day or night. Except for drug stuff several years ago, his record is clean. As far as anything we can find, he's not been in any kind of trouble, drugs or otherwise, for the past three years. We can't haul him in for being on city streets."

"But you hear so much . . . " Grams says.

"I know. It *is* a worry. It sounds like more than coincidence that he keeps showing up. But it's nothing to arrest the guy on, or even question him about. Now if he were to approach you, Lauren, that would be a different story."

"If we wait until he approaches her, it may be too late," Grams says.

Dennis turns to me. "The thing for you to do is to be extremely cautious. Don't walk anywhere alone, even in broad daylight. Stay off the streets as much as you can. You need to go somewhere — drive, or have someone drive you. It may be nothing. But *act* as if there's a murderer/rapist out to get you."

"Can't you offer some protection?" Grams says.

"Sorry. I guess you could hire a *private* bodyguard, but we don't have the personnel to do it. I wish I could be of more help."

Grams nods her head sadly. "I wish you could, too."

"I'll talk with Amber — see if her description matches the owner of the Honda. I'll talk with Ms. Woods, and I'll alert everyone at the station to a possible problem with this guy. That's the best I can do."

"Do you think the phone calls are related?" Grams asks.

Dennis shrugs. "Maybe. Maybe not. You got an answering machine?"

"No. I hate them," Grams says.

"Well . . . you should get one. At least until we know what's going on here. Get a machine and never pick up the phone until you hear who it is on the other end."

"It seems so rude," Grams says.

"Tell your friends what you're doing. They'll understand. Usually prank callers get tired of answering machines pretty damned quick."

Grams sighs.

"Also, call the phone company and get set up with Caller I.D."

"What?"

"Caller Identification. It'll flash the caller's number, so if you recognize it, you can pick right up. If you don't, you can write it down and maybe we can find out who's calling."

Grams looks doubtful.

"It's easy," Dennis says.

Grams and Dennis stand talking at the door for a while before he leaves. How're the kids, what do you hear from Claudia, that sort of thing. I guess Grams first met him when he and Aunt Claudia were dating. He doesn't seem her type, but I remember she once told me, you've got to kiss a lot of frogs before you find your prince. I wonder if the sheriff was one of the frogs she kissed. I don't mean that in an insulting way. He seems like a nice guy — just nothing like Uncle Malcolm, who's this brainy, witty guy who looks like a young Sean Connery.

When Tyler comes to get me, Grams tries to talk us into staying home instead of going to whatever is left of the game. She even tries to bribe us with hot fudge sundaes.

"I'd at least like to see the last half," Tyler says.

"Me, too," I chime in.

"Oh, I know. You can't hide under a rock. And you're both sensible kids. This thing just has me so on edge."

"I won't let Lauren out of my sight," Tyler tells Grams.

"*Please*, let me know if you're going to be late. I can't help worrying."

I give Grams a long hug and we're out the door. Tyler walks to the sidewalk and looks up and down in both directions.

"No red Honda around right now," he says.

We get to the game at halftime and make our way over to where Blake is sitting with Megan and Kelsey. It is cool out, but comfortable. A light wind has sweetened and lightened the air, and the band sounds better than usual. It's one of those times that feels right. I guess I'm just happy to be here with Tyler and my friends, and to not think about the red Honda for a while.

As soon as I sit down, Blake climbs over Kelsey and scoots in between us.

He puts his hand beside his mouth and whispers, "I called her."

"I know," I say back.

"Shhh!"

"What, are you ashamed?"

"No, I just don't want jabbering Kelsey to start spreading rumors . . . She likes me," Blake says, a big grin plastered across his face. "She laughed in the right places."

"You sure jump to conclusions. Just because Amber has a sense of humor doesn't mean she's fallen for *you*."

"Uh, huh," he says. "She likes me. You know she likes me. What'd she say?"

"You're the man of her dreams," I tell him.

"Really? Really???"

"No," I say, laughing. "But she sounded happy about going out with you."

"Awesome."

"She thought you were funny and sweet."

"Sweet?" Tyler says, practically choking on his soda.

"I didn't even think you were listening," I say.

He puts his arm around me.

"When *you* talk, I *listen*."

Our laughter is drowned out by the huge cheer that greets the Hamilton High team as they run back onto the field. They're only behind by two touchdowns, which is *good* for Hamilton High, so our side is enthusiastic.

During a lull in the game I tell Tyler about the visit to the Habitat for Humanity house, and how Shawna said she could get some camellias.

"Good idea," Tyler says.

"Will you help us with the planting?"

"If I get to be the design boss."

"No problem," I say.

After the game we all pile into Tyler's car and go to Barb 'n Edie's. That place is so crowded we can't even get through the door. We hang around outside for a while, joking with the blue and gold crowd. Finally we give up on ever getting inside Barb 'n Edie's and go to Manny's for burritos. Kelsey tries to sell Manny an ad in *Connections,* but he tells her to come back when he's not so busy.

"You should follow through," Megan says.

"I will! Do you think I'm stupid or something?"

There's a long pause, while Megan sits grinning.

"Your silence speaks volumes," Blake says.

That gets Tyler going with his snorty laugh, and we all get hysterical. Manny watches us like we're crazy, which we sort of are for now.

"I don't see what's so funny," Kelsey says, which increases the volume of our laughter by about a hundred decibels.

After Tyler drops everyone else off at their houses, we drive a few miles into the next city and park on a kind of dead end street in the middle of a big, private, college campus. There are no street lights here, and never any traffic either. It was at this place, on a dark, moonless night like tonight, that Tyler and I first realized we loved each other in a special way.

"I know it's not our anniversary yet, but I want to give you your present early."

"But I don't even have yours yet," I tell him.

"I know. I can wait for mine. I just can't wait for yours."

Even though it's almost totally dark, I'm sure Tyler has that big grin he gets on his face when he's happy about something.

"Okay," I say, never one to turn down an early gift.

He takes a wadded-up handkerchief from his jacket pocket and very carefully unwraps it. He opens the car door a bit, so the light will come on, and takes a broad silver ring from the middle of the hanky.

"Look, this is so neat," he says.

He gives the ring a twist and it separates into two rings.

"See, it's got this little lock thing that makes the two parts fit together perfectly. Like you and me."

"They're beautiful," I say, running my finger across the smooth, polished surface.

"Last summer, I saw them in a store at the mall and right away I started saving money from my paycheck."

"I love you so much," I tell him. "I can't believe how lucky I am, that you love me, too."

"I'm the lucky one," he says, kissing me in a gentle, tender way.

He puts one part of the ring on the fourth finger of my right hand.

"We'll save your left ring finger for later, like we're saving other things for later."

He tries to put the other half of the ring on his right ring finger, but his finger's too big. He ends up with it on his little finger on his left hand.

"That works," he says, putting his left hand on top of my right, so the rings are close to each other.

"The guy at the jewelry store said it could be a friendship ring, or a promise ring."

"Which is it for us?" I ask.

"I promise to always, always, love you," Tyler says.

"I promise to always, always, love you, too," I say.

Tyler closes the car door so the light goes out. We recline our seats as far back as they'll go. He holds me close and we kiss again, harder, deeper, and then our hands are all over each other, excited, reaching for special places, moving faster, breathing harder, helping each other feel good. Better. Best!

We stay close, arms around each other, Tyler's head nuzzled against my neck. He strokes my cheek. My hand rests on his upper arm and I feel the hardness of his biceps under his shirt sleeve. I'd like to stay like this forever, but soon the night air grows cold. We rearrange our clothes and put our seats back in their regular positions.

"Tyler?"

"Curly?" he says, gently pulling at a strand of hair.

"I'm so relieved, that you're okay with the true love waits thing."

"Well . . . I've thought about it a lot," he says. "I don't want to have that experience with you unless you want it, too. Anytime you're ready — wow! That would make me the happiest guy in the world. But no more pressure from me. That's not what I'm about."

At times like this I'm so filled with love for Tyler I can hardly stand it. I'm beaming at him. I can tell. My smile is so big my cheeks ache.

Then Tyler gets this worried frown.

"Lauren, I . . . "

He looks at me for a long time. Whatever he starts to say, he changes his mind. He starts the car and we head back toward my house.

I look down at the ring on my finger, and on the other half of the ring on Tyler's finger. I think of the promise the rings stand for, and I've never in my whole life felt so loved or so happy.

16

I'm barely out of bed Sunday morning when Tyler calls.

"Did you sleep with your ring on last night?" he asks.

"I'll never take it off."

"Me either, except maybe to polish it now and then . . . Hey, listen. Shawna called me this morning to talk about the Habitat house plants."

"She did?"

"Yeah. She'd talked to Mr. Schaefer about all those dying plants. He said sure, take them. The only thing is, he wants them cleared out today, otherwise he plans to dump them and clear out that space."

"I've got Jackie's phone number. Shall I call her and see if we can work over there this afternoon?"

"Yeah, that'd be good. Mr. Schaefer said I could use one of the nursery trucks if we'd get that stuff out today."

"I'll call Jackie and then call you right back."

Luckily, Jackie is home.

"You kids sure work fast!" she says. "There'll be someone working inside, so you can use the bathroom if you need to. No organized lunch there today, though. You're on your own in the food department."

I call Tyler back and tell him we can get started.

"We're going to need all the help we can get with the planting. That stuff should go in the ground as soon as possible. Will Amber help? And your gramma?"

"Grams?"

"We need people who know what they're doing — no offense to you and Amber," he says with that laugh of his.

I pick up Amber and we go to the nursery to help load plants onto the truck.

"Wait!" she says as we round the corner of the storage shed. She backs up and pulls me back with her.

"What's *he* doing here?" she whispers.

"Blake?" I whisper back.

"Yeah, *Blake*! Is this some kind of trap?"

"I didn't even know he was going to be here. Tyler probably called him to help. What's the big deal?"

"I said I'd go out with him Saturday night, with you and Tyler. I didn't say I'd be hanging out with him from here on out."

"Come on, Amber, get . . ."

Blake turns the corner of the shed and practically runs into us. He backs up, looking at Amber.

"Hi," he says.

"Hi," she says back.

Blake walks to the side of the building and picks up some bungee cords, then goes back the way he came.

"See, that was uneventful," I tell Amber. "Come on."

We walk behind the shed, where Tyler and Blake are loading plants on the truck. Shawna is in the back of the truck, arranging plants as they lift them up to her. There's a lot more than camellias.

"Look," Tyler says. "Two little orange trees and a lime, too."

"That's really nice of your boss," I say.

"It's a tax write-off for him. He couldn't sell any of this stuff, anyway," Shawna says, all cynical.

"Never one to see the bright side, are you?" Tyler laughs.

To my surprise, Shawna laughs, too.

Amber and I go over to an area where there are about twenty scrawny plants lined up.

"Do these go?" I ask Tyler.

"Everything except the big fern at the end."

"Mr. Schaefer said the fern could go, too," Shawna says.

"You sure?" Tyler asks.

Shawna nods her head.

"I'm just going to check," Tyler says, running into the old office to use the phone.

Amber and I carry the plants to the truck bed and hand them up to Shawna. The citrus trees aren't very big, for trees, but they're still hard to wrestle onto the truck.

Tyler comes out of the office, closing the rickety door behind him.

"Okay, load the fern, too."

"Told you," Shawna says, displaying the faintest of smiles.

Finally, when everything is loaded, Tyler and Shawna and Blake get in the truck to go to the Habitat place, and Amber and I go back to my house to pick up Grams.

When we get to the Habitat house the truck is already unloaded.

"We'll plant all this stuff in the back," Tyler says. "Then, in another month or so we can get material for the front."

By the time Tyler has finished his sentence, Grams has grabbed her gloves and tools from the trunk of her car and started working the soil near the side fence.

"We could space these camellias out in a kind of border along this ugly chain link fence, don't you think, Tyler? It'll give it a lot of color when the bushes get bigger."

He laughs. "Why did I ask your gramma to help if I wanted to be the design boss?" he says to me.

"You got a better idea?" Grams says with a smile.

"Well, no," Tyler says.

Grams starts moving the camellias over by the fence, where she thinks they should be planted.

Blake unloads bags of potting soil and cedar chips.

"Did Schaefer say we could have those, too?" Shawna asks Tyler.

"Yep," Tyler says.

Grams digs a hole for the first camellia.

"Just do it the way your gramma does," Tyler says.

Amber and I go over by the fence and dig holes for the next two bushes.

"The hole needs to be about three times as big as the plant's root system. That way you can add plenty of good soil mix, so the roots will have good stuff to grow into."

Amber and I make the holes bigger. Then, with more advice from Grams, we add the soil mix, ease the plants from their pots, then into the holes, add more soil mix, then water, and finally add cedar chips to the top.

"That helps keep moisture in and the soil temperature more even, so the roots won't freeze in the winter or burn in the summer."

"How do you know so much?" Amber asks.

"I'm old," Grams says. "Haven't you heard of the wisdom of the ages?"

Even though there are six of us working, it's nearly dark by the time we get everything planted. It all looks pretty scraggly. I'm not sure any of it will live, but Tyler and Grams are convinced it will.

"Lauren and I can stop by in the middle of the week to see if anything needs watering," Tyler says.

"Sure," I say.

"I can do that easy," Shawna says. "I live just around the corner."

Grams offers to take us all to Barb 'n Edie's — an offer no one refuses. We load tools and empty pots back onto the truck, then take turns in the bathrooms, scrubbing our hands clear up to our elbows.

When I go to get into Grams' car, Amber and Blake are already there.

"I decided to leave room for you so you could ride with Tyler in the truck," Blake says. "Nice guy, huh?"

"Yeah. What a sacrifice for you to ride with Amber."

We laugh, then I climb into the truck beside Tyler and Shawna gets in after me.

"This is great," Tyler says as he backs out of the driveway. "I know where I can get some river rock to put in over by the patio, next to the lime tree. It'll add visual interest."

Shawna starts talking about a "water feature."

"You mean a fountain?" I ask.

"Yeah, or a kind of riverbed look, just touched by water on the surface."

"Like at that demo garden we saw on the video?" Tyler asks.

"Yeah. How hard would that be?"

"Not hard, but expensive."

They start talking about how something like that might be put together. They both seem to know a lot about things I've never even thought about.

"The kids'd probably tear up one of those riverbed things in no time," Shawna says.

"Not necessarily," Tyler says. "Stop thinking the worst."

"The world is full of worst," Shawna says, falling back into her old posture with her hair hiding her face.

"And the best," Tyler says, reaching for my hand and rubbing his thumb across my ring, smiling.

It's easy to get into Barb 'n Edie's on a Sunday evening.

"Order whatever you want," Grams says. "I just won the lottery."

"Really?" Shawna asks, all astounded like.

"No," Grams smiles. "Just pretend I did."

Shawna smiles back at Grams, a nice, un-Shawna-like smile.

Blake and Amber and Shawna sit on one side of the table, and Grams and Tyler and I sit on the other. We talk about the whole Habitat for Humanity project, and how important it is for people to help each other out. Grams tells stories she'd heard from her father, about how people shared their food during the depression. Blake tells about the old guy who lives next door to him, who volunteers at a homeless shelter, keeping it clean and helping out wherever he can. I watch Amber watching Blake as he talks. I think he's right. She likes him.

It is warm and bright here in Barb 'n Edie's, and, having worked hard all day, the food is even more tasty than usual. I have that feeling again, like I had at the football game last night, that everything is right, and that I belong. I glance at Shawna, who's folding and refolding a paper napkin. I'll bet she doesn't even know she's doing it. I wonder if *she* ever gets that feeling, that everything is right, and that she belongs. Sometimes I feel so sorry for her, and other times she annoys me to pieces.

Once, just before we leave, I think I get a glimpse of the red Honda driving slowly by. Even that doesn't take away my feeling of well-being.

As we leave Barb 'n Edie's Tyler grabs my hand and squeezes three times. I squeeze back. He gives me a quick, okay-for-Grams to see, peck on the cheek.

"Call you later," he says.

"Okay."

He and Blake and Shawna get in the truck to take it back to the nursery.

Grams and I take Amber home, then go home ourselves.

"You have such nice friends," Grams tells me.

"Not like Marcia," I say.

"Not at all."

"What about Shawna?" I ask.

"What I think about Shawna is that she's developed a very hard shell for some reason or another, but that she's very kindhearted on the inside. Is that what you think?"

"Maybe," I say. "I'm getting to like her some, now that I'm getting to know her."

"Tell me this, though. It looks as if your friend Amber's found a boyfriend."

"Was it obvious?"

Grams just smiles — then suddenly her expression changes.

"Oh, goodness," she says.

"What?"

"I just remembered, I've got several shovels that belong to the nursery in the trunk of my car. Remember, we were keeping them there because it was handy?"

I glance at the clock. "I'll take them back. If I hurry, I'll bet they'll still be there," I say, happy for an excuse to see Tyler one more time.

"I don't think that's what Dennis meant when he said to observe extreme caution."

"Oh, Grams. I'll stay in the car with the doors locked. I won't even get *out* unless Tyler's still at the nursery. It'll be okay," I assure her.

"Well . . . be back in thirty minutes or I'm calling the police," she says, tossing me her keys.

17

When I get to the nursery I'm happy to see that Tyler's car is still there. The tools and empty pots have been unloaded from the truck bed, but no one seems to be around. They've got to be here somewhere, though. I park next to Tyler's car and walk through rows of plants. There is a bright security light out front, but I can barely see where I'm going here in the dark. It is dead quiet.

"Tyler!" I yell.

No answer. Where can they be? I hear a car on the street and wonder if it's the red Honda. I walk faster. Maybe they're using the phone or something. I'm almost running now, to the old office, where I see a dim light.

I stop at the window, cup my hands and look inside. I can barely see, but I see too much.

Shawna is on her back, on the ratty couch, with Tyler on top. His bare butt shows white in the faint light. His jeans are down around his thighs. An empty foil condom wrapper lies crumpled on the floor. I am frozen at the window, wanting not to look, unable to turn away. Shawna's bare legs are wrapped around

Tyler's ankles and he is pushing, pushing, pushing until the spell is broken by his groan of pleasure. The sound no one else was supposed to hear.

"No!" I scream. "No! No!"

Tyler looks up quickly, startled, and I turn and run. I jump into the car, slam it into reverse, peel backward, slam it into drive and spin gravel to the gate.

"LAUREN!" I hear Tyler's frantic call, and press harder on the accelerator.

In my mirror I see him standing in the driveway, holding his unfastened pants up with one hand and waving frantically with the other. I know he is yelling at the top of his lungs, but the sound of my pushed-to-the-limit engine drowns him out.

Tears stream down my face.

"No! No! Why? Why?"

I yell all the way home, to no one, and turn into the driveway without slowing. I jam on the brakes and squeal to a stop, inches from the closed garage door. I run into the back door and collide with Grams, who is rushing to meet me.

"What is it?" she asks. "The red car — was he chasing you? I'm calling Dennis right now."

"No, it's not that," I manage to gasp.

I squeeze past Grams and run into my bedroom, my safe place, and flop face down on the bed.

Grams follows right behind. "What is it? What is it?"

I shake my head, sobbing.

"Did you see the red car?"

I shake my head.

"Were you in an accident? Is someone hurt?"

I shake my head again, heaving so hard with sobs it seems I could break apart. Grams gives my shoulders a shake.

"Lauren, you've got to talk to me! I can't help you if you won't talk!"

But I know she can't help anyway, and I can't talk. I can't put words to it. I can only cry. And cry. And cry.

Grams sits on my bed, next to me, for a long time, rubbing my back. Finally, my sobs subside.

"Can I get you anything? A cup of tea, maybe?"

I shake my head.

"Well, I think *I* could use a cup of tea," Grams says.

When she's gone, I turn over and look around my room. It's strange, how the whole world can change but things still look the same. I yank off the promise ring and throw it against the window. It bounces off the glass and lands on my desk. I turn my face to the wall and curl up, tight. I don't want to feel. I don't want to think.

"Lauren? . . . Lauren?" My grandmother is calling to me. It sounds as if she's calling from a distance, even though she is sitting on my bed and rubbing my back.

"Tyler's here. He wants to see you."

"No!"

"He's upset."

"No!!" I say, trying to curl tighter, into a smaller ball.

I hear mumbling in the other room but I make myself not hear. I don't want to hear words — especially not Tyler's words. I concentrate on hearing my own breathing, sensing the emptiness within me.

Sometime late, when there are no traffic noises in the distance, Grams comes into my room. I pretend to be asleep. She puts her gentle, cool hand on my forehead, as if I might have a fever. What I have, though, is the opposite of a fever. There is no warmth in me now, only a deep, silent, chill.

Grams leaves, and I breathe, empty, through the night. Mostly I'm in a place without thought, but sometimes a question breaks through. Why? What happened? How did he stop loving me so fast? And with Shawna??? Mark was right when he called her a dog. Doggie Shawna. How could Tyler do that to me?

I open my eyes with the early morning light. Except for the ring at the edge of my desk, taunting me, everything still looks the same — my same, safe room. The ring can stay right where it is, a reminder that there are no true promises. I learned that a long time ago, when Marcia promised to make a life for us when she got out of prison. All those broken promises written on prison issue lined paper. There are no true promises. I forgot that for a while, with Tyler. I won't forget again.

Grams comes in early in the morning.

"I want to talk with you before you go to school," she says.

"I'm not going to school."

"Are you sick?"

"Yes."

I am sick at the thought of walking into creative writing and sitting next to Shawna and Tyler in our Habitat group, as if nothing has happened. I am sick at the thought of seeing them in class, and worse, of seeing them in my mind together, and hearing his moan of pleasure.

I am sick.

Grams leaves and comes back with a cup of tea for each of us. She sets mine on my bedside table, then sits in my desk chair, facing me. She picks up the "promise" ring, then sets it down.

"I don't know what's upset you so," Grams says. "I know it has something to do with Tyler, and I know he's plenty upset, too."

She takes a sip of tea and sits watching me. I keep my eye on the bird feeder outside the window, somewhere over and beyond Grams' right shoulder.

"Talking might help," she says.

"It won't."

"You might be surprised."

I've already been surprised, I think. I don't want to talk about it. I turn back with my face to the wall. For a while I hear Grams taking sips of tea. Then, eventually, she sighs and leaves the room.

Sometime when the sun is shining softly on the pansies in the flower bed outside my window, I hear Grams on the phone.

"No. I'm sorry, I can't be there today... My granddaughter is ill... Well, you'll just have to find a substitute for the substitute I guess."

Later in the morning Grams comes to my door to offer soft boiled eggs, which is what I always used to eat when I was sick.

"No, thanks."

She feels my forehead again. "No fever. But maybe I should call Dr. Lee, anyway."

"No," I say.

She gives me one of those long, appraising looks, then walks back out to the kitchen. I hear her fussing around out there as I drift back to my breathing, thoughtless state.

Afternoon, I hear the murmur of voices in the kitchen and rouse myself enough to listen a bit. It is Grams' friend, Betty.

"Do you know what has her so spooked?"

"Love, I think, but I'm not sure."

"What a mess of things the creator made when she set women up with that love-need."

"Oh, I'm not so sure about that," Grams says. "There's lots that's wonderful there. Lots of pleasure."

"Lots of pain," Betty says.

I'm on Betty's side with this one.

"Thanks for picking this up for me, Betty. Maybe it's silly, but I didn't want to leave Lauren alone and go off on errands."

"No trouble," Betty says. "I got you the same kind I've got, so I can help you set it up."

I hear them tearing a carton apart and realize Grams is following her sheriff friend's advice about an answering machine. Yesterday that would have made me so happy, because it would have meant I'd always know when Tyler called, even if no one was home. Today? Rip the phone out for all I care.

After Betty leaves, Grams suggests I come out and see the machine, and she'll show me how it works.

"No thanks," I say, which is also what I say later, when she asks if I want dinner, and later still, when she tells me Amber's on the phone and asks if I want to talk to her. It's the same answer I've given each time Tyler's called today. No thanks. I don't want to talk to him. I don't want to think about him. I don't want to see him with Shawna, over and over again, in my head, a constantly repeating scene set in the nursery office.

Late in the evening, after Grams shuts off the evening news, I hear her walking down the hall toward my room. I turn my face to the wall, again pretending sleep. Grams opens the door and walks to the side of my bed. I guess she thinks I'm sick enough, or weird enough, that knocking is no longer appropriate. I don't stir. I can feel her looking down on me. She nudges my shoulder.

"Lauren?"

I don't respond.

She nudges again, more insistently.

"Lauren!"

"What?" I mumble.

"Listen, Lauren. You haven't eaten all day. You're still in the same clothes you were in when you came home last night. I know something awful must have happened, but I don't know what. You've either got to talk with me about it, or you've got to work to get past it. You can't have another day like today. If you're not up in the morning and eating a little breakfast, you're going to the doctor," Grams says, then walks out, closing the door behind her.

I'm sorry if I've worried her, or made her mad. I just don't know how to be anymore. I don't know how to be in the world, with the image of Tyler and Shawna always there, right behind my eyes. I don't see how I can possibly get out of bed in the morning, or eat anything. I've got to stay here, in my room, tucked away, where I'm safe.

Tuesday morning I force myself to get up and shower and eat a few spoonfuls of cereal and drink a glass of orange juice. Enough to convince Grams that I don't need a doctor.

"Take the car to school today," she says. "I don't need it until this evening, and I'll feel safer knowing you're not walking around where the red Honda can find you."

"Okay," I say.

I feel like my whole being is sunk to the size of a walnut and it's hiding in the deepest part of my body it can find, somewhere between my belly button and my spine — a tiny me.

"You still don't look very chipper," Grams says.

"I'll be okay," I tell her, but in my heart I know that's not true.

I pick up my backpack and get into the car, as if I'm going to school. I do drive *past* the school, slowly. There is Tyler, sitting on the bench, looking toward the parking lot as if he's waiting for someone. As if he's waiting for me. As if the whole world weren't changed.

It is a gray morning, gray sky, gray outlines of mountains, gray air, all the more gray when seen through tears. I drive to the foothills, park, and walk. The hundreds of times I've walked this path guide my steps. Step after step, trying to think, then trying not to think. Think. Don't think.

I walk past Baby Hope's bush, on to the waterfall. There hasn't been much rain lately, and the waterfall is more of a trickle than a fall. The pool below is shallow and muddy. I pick up one of the heaviest river rocks I can lift and smash it down into the mud, pretending it is smashing into Shawna's face. Rock after rock. Smash Shawna. Smash Shawna — time after time, until my arms are so tired I can't lift another rock. Nothing works. Nothing makes things better.

I walk to the peak and sit near the edge of the trail, looking down on the valley below. Not much can be seen on a day like this. It is murky, like the pool at the waterfall, like my soul.

On my way down I pause at Baby Hope's bush. I get out my journal and sit down, ready to write. But all I can think of is why. Why? Why? When everything was so good. Tears come again. It seems I should be empty of tears by now, but they keep coming. I start taking deep breaths, to calm myself, but that reminds me of Tyler, how he taught me to do that, and I cry even harder. I won't think of it anymore, I tell myself. I won't think of them, there in the office. But as soon as I think that, their image, Tyler on Shawna, overwhelms me.

Sometime in the afternoon, by the bush, my mind goes back to the tiny Baby Hope on the trail, blue and barely breathing, and then to seeing Grams breathing into her, a pinkish tone gradually coming to the baby's face, and for a moment Baby Hope coming alive overcomes the scene from the dimly lit office of the nursery.

As I walk through our back door, the phone is ringing and Grams is hovering over it, reading the displayed number.

"It's so hard to remember not to answer the phone," she tells me. "I've been answering the phone all my life, and now . . . "

Tyler's voice comes on, "I really have to talk to you, Lauren.

I can explain everything. Call me when you get home."

I press the erase button and walk back to my bedroom. In just a few minutes the phone rings again. This time it is Amber.

"An answering machine? Welcome to the twenty-first century. Call me. Where were you today, anyway?"

Grams opens my bedroom door. "Amber asked where you were — didn't you go to school today?"

"No."

"Why not?"

"I just couldn't," I sigh.

"Lauren, I know you can't always share your personal secrets with me, but if you're in trouble, let me help."

"Oh, Grams, no one can help."

"Well . . . whatever it is, as awful as it may seem, you've still got to go to school."

"I know," I say. "I just can't stand to see Tyler right now."

"He said he could explain," Grams says. "Maybe you should give him a chance."

"I can't."

"But he's such a nice young man . . . "

"Oh, Grams," I say, letting my voice show annoyance.

After a long silence, Grams asks, "Pizza sound good for tonight?"

"Sure," I say.

"The usual?"

"Sure."

I know she's trying to make me feel better. Pizza always used to work, if my team had lost at soccer, or I'd messed up on a spelling test. Pizza was good for that. The sadness I'm feeling now is bigger than pizza, though.

The phone rings again. This time, no one leaves a message.

I open *Jane Eyre* and read of her terrible loneliness and despair at having had to be separated from Mr. Rochester. She wishes she had died in the night, but then she thinks,

"Life, however, was yet in my possession: with all its

requirements, and pains, and responsibilities. The burden must be carried; the want provided for; the suffering endured, the responsibility fulfilled."

I guess that's one way to look at things right now. Life is a burden that must be carried. I must eat my pizza, and go to school, and do everything I've done before. Everything but love Tyler. Everything but trust that promises can be kept. I guess that still leaves me being one of the "everything but" girls. Except now I don't know what the "everything" stands for. It seems more like nothing is left.

Amber comes over, unannounced, as Grams and I are finishing dinner.

"Oh, Amber. I'm glad you're here. It's our Scrabble night at Betty's, and I'd feel better about going if Lauren weren't left all alone."

"I'll babysit," Amber says with a laugh.

I force a smile, then start clearing the table.

As soon as Grams is out the door, Amber says, "Tell me everything!"

"I really don't want to talk about it," I say.

"What happened, anyway?" Amber asks, as if she's not even heard that I don't want to talk.

I shake my head.

"Tyler keeps telling me 'I've got to talk to Lauren. Get Lauren to talk to me,' like his vocabulary is limited to about ten words."

As if on cue, the phone rings and it's Tyler, leaving the same message. "Talk to me, Lauren."

"Aren't you going to pick up?" Amber says.

"No."

"When are you going to talk to him?"

"Never."

"Lauren! How can you do that? He's the love of your life, remember?"

"That's what I thought. I was wrong."

"But everything was fine at the Habitat house. What happened?"

As much as I don't want to talk about it, I hear myself start the story, slowly at first, and then as fast as the words will come.

"You're sure?" Amber asks, eyes wide with surprise.

"Sure."

"Tyler with Shawna? Doing it? In the nursery office? Are you serious?"

"Do I look like I'm joking?"

"Unbelievable!"

"Believe it," I say.

I tell Amber about going to the foothills, and smashing Shawna's pretend face with giant rocks.

"Why Shawna?"

"Why SHAWNA??"

I am amazed that Amber can ask such a stupid question.

"No, I mean, why not Tyler? He's the one to be mad at."

"But if it weren't for Shawna none of this would have happened."

"He's a guy. There'd have been someone else."

"I guess."

"But he had me fooled, too. Tyler was the last guy I thought would do something like that," Amber says. "You're *sure* you saw what you thought you saw? You said it was really dark."

"I'm sure, Amber. I'm as sure as I can be. Don't ask me that again."

The phone rings again. We listen. This time it's Shawna.

"Lauren, I need to talk to you. I can explain."

"This is weird," Amber says. "You should hear what *she* has to say. And you should at least give Tyler a chance. I mean, he's been like the perfect guy. Maybe there *is* some explanation, like they were just pretending or something."

"Amber. I *know* what I saw."

"Okay. Okay. It's just so unbelievable, that's all."

There are three more phone calls before Amber leaves. One for Grams and two from Tyler. I erase the ones from Tyler.

"Shall I pick you up for school in the morning?" Amber says. "I'm sure I can borrow Mom's car tomorrow."

"Yeah, okay," I say.

"Coach Terry was mad to the highest power that you weren't there yesterday or today. Better be prepared for a lecture, especially after she finds out today was unexcused."

"I dread going to school," I say.

"I'll stay right beside you all day tomorrow. You don't want to talk to people? — I'll block them."

She shows me her special jump-up-and-down-in-front-of-my- face conversation block. I feel myself smile for the first time in days.

"I'll even go to creative writing with you if you want me to."

"Thanks," I say, realizing what a good friend Amber truly is.

"Hey. You've always been there for me. I'll be there for you, Kinky Sister."

"Okay, Sister Blondie," I say, smiling again.

The smiles don't keep me from crying myself to sleep later, when the house is quiet and dark. I'm still as sad as I've ever been. But talking with Amber helped some. Not that anything has changed, but that the burden is shared. If only I could get out of going to school tomorrow, seeing Shawna, seeing Tyler, seeing the night-time scene replayed again and again. I don't know if I can do that or not.

CHAPTER

Amber parks in the lot on the north side of the school, as far away from where Tyler always parks as possible. She grabs her backpack, gets out of the car and slams the door. I sit in the car. She comes around to the other side and opens the door.

"Well?" she says.

"I can't do it."

"Come on. It's only school."

"No. It's Tyler and Shawna this period."

"You can't just keep cutting class."

"I'm NOT going to go to creative writing and sit in the same room with Shawna and Tyler, and pretend nothing happened!"

"Okay. Okay. Stay there. I'll come back and walk with you to peer communications."

I shake my head. "Don't you see? I really can't see Shawna."

"Well, I'll see you in English then."

I nod. Amber closes the car door and walks away toward her zero period. I take *Jane Eyre* from my backpack and find the spot where I left off. Jane Eyre was cold and hungry and had no place to stay since she left Mr. Rochester's. She sat in the driving rain, waiting to die. I'm sitting in a warm car. I've had breakfast and I have a home to go to. But I believe I am as sad and desolate as Jane Eyre ever was. Should that make me feel better, knowing my feelings are so common that a woman way back in the nineteenth century could write about the same emotions? I try to look at things philosophically. Many people suffer terrible disappointments in love. Why should I expect anything different? But it's all theory, and I feel just as lost and empty inside as ever.

I notice when it's time for English, notice the bell and students milling around between classes. I slump down in the car, so no one will see me. Second period passes. Then third.

Amber comes to the car and tries to talk me into at least going to afternoon classes. I say yes, but I don't leave the car until time for volleyball practice. It will do me good to hit the ball, and I don't have to worry about seeing Tyler or Shawna there.

Coach Terry lectures me way too long about missing practice, then I take my place on the court. It's still Marcia I serve, but now it's Shawna I spike. Wham! Down to the ground! Smash that face! Once, when I'm set up for a perfect spike, I try to turn the ball into Tyler's face.

"Hey, keep your mind on the game!" Coach Terry yells when the ball bounces lightly off my fingers and lands outside the boundaries.

Practice is nearly over when Shawna comes walking onto the court, heavy flannel shirt, baggy jeans, head down.

"Hey, off the court! What's going on here?" Coach Terry yells.

Shawna keeps walking, straight toward me. She stops right in front of me, throws her hair back so I can see those gray-blue eyes.

"I've got to talk to you!" she says, loud and firm, in a voice I've never heard.

The scene from the nursery flashes before me and my head is spinning with Shawna, her face, her presence. I haul back and slam my open hand into her face, aiming it over the net, but it goes nowhere. I haul back again but someone blocks my arm. Coach Terry, Amber, the rest of the team, swarm around us. Amber is in front of me, blocking Shawna.

"No! Stop!" she's yelling right in my face.

I jump high, trying to pull my arm loose, to spike Shawna, but I can't reach her.

Coach Terry has Shawna by the arm, pulling her away.

"I've got to talk to you, you stupid bitch!" Shawna yells.

"Let me go!" I yell to whoever it is holding my arms, pulling at my waist, but the pressure only tightens. I struggle to squirm away, to get at Shawna, but they've got me.

Two security guys come running over, one grabbing me by the shoulders and the other grabbing Shawna. Their walkie-talkies are squawking and a crowd is gathering. Across the courts I see Tyler running toward us.

We're already being led away to the vice principal's office by the time he joins the crowd. My last glimpse of him is with Amber, talking intently.

"**W**hat's this about?" Dr. Ogden asks, motioning us to sit down.

Coach Terry sits between me and Shawna. The two security guys stay standing, one next to Shawna and the other next to me. My hands are trembling and it's everything I can do not to cry.

"Terry?"

"This young woman, Shawna, came walking onto the volleyball court in the middle of practice. She defiantly refused to leave, engaged in a fight with my student, used foul language, and tried to fight off security."

"Do you have anything to add?" Dr. Ogden says, looking from one security guard to the other.

Both shake their heads.

Dr. Ogden's secretary comes in carrying two big file folders and sets them down on his desk, then leaves. One of the folders has my name on it and the other has Shawna's. Our permanent records, I suppose. Shawna's is about twice as thick as mine.

"What is the meaning of this, Shawna?" Dr. Ogden asks.

Shawna is hidden behind her hair and doesn't answer. I wonder what her cheek looks like under that mass of hair. My hand, the one I hit her with, is red and throbbing.

"Do you have anything to add, Lauren?" Dr. Ogden says.

I shake my head.

"So this is the version we're going with?"

"I was right there," Coach Terry says. "Lauren was minding her own business when Shawna came looking for trouble."

Dr. Ogden shakes his head sadly as he thumbs through Shawna's file, looking at referral after referral.

"Well . . . Harry, will you sit with Shawna in the office for a few minutes, until I'm finished here with Lauren?"

They leave. Then Dr. Ogden gives Coach Terry and the other security guy each forms to fill out, and they leave. Dr. Ogden opens my folder and leafs through the pages, stopping now and then to read more thoroughly.

"Now, Lauren, I can see from your permanent record that you are not a trouble maker. But anytime there's an event of violence, all parties must have at least a one-day suspension. So you'll stay home from school tomorrow, even though you obviously were not the aggressor. "

I could tell him I'd treated Shawna's head like a volleyball, but I don't.

"Shawna will be transferred to a more appropriate placement, since this is just one of a long string of difficulties she's had here."

I tuck my hands under my legs, trying to control the trembling.

"I'm only telling you what will happen with Shawna because I don't want you to be afraid to return," Dr. Ogden says.

He and Coach Terry have totally misinterpreted the whole thing. But that's what happens a lot with the adults around here. They don't quite get it.

But what does it matter? Nothing matters. I half listen to Dr. Ogden's advice while I pay more attention to the pain in my hand. I'm glad my hand hurts. It's a distraction from the deeper hurts inside me.

I'm only about three blocks from school, walking home, when I think I get a glimpse of the red Honda. I don't care, I just keep walking. Then, about half way home, I hear the familiar sound of Tyler's car. I don't turn to look. The car stops, engine shuts off. I keep walking, faster, head down.

"Lauren! Lauren!"

I don't answer him.

"I've got to talk with you. You don't understand!"

I'm running now, Tyler close behind me. He catches me by my arm, pulls me around to face him.

"You've got to listen!"

I jerk free and run ahead. Again he catches me, this time holding me with both arms. I pull away, hard, but he hangs on harder. His face is troubled, intent.

"It's not . . ."

The red Honda slams to a stop on the sidewalk right in front of us. The driver jumps out of the car and hurls himself at Tyler.

"Leave her alone!" he demands, grabbing Tyler and throwing him to the sidewalk.

"Come on," he says, trying to pull me into his car.

"No!" I scream.

Tyler is up again, pulling with all his might at the man's large, hard-muscled arms, freeing me.

"Run, Lauren! Run!"

For one paralyzed moment I look at Tyler, see the man effortlessly free himself, hear the thud of Tyler's body slam into the sidewalk as the man again starts toward me. Fear rushes through me and I run for all I'm worth. Footsteps are behind me, not the light fleet footsteps of Tyler Bronson, but the heavy, pounding footsteps of the red Honda man, gaining.

"Rennie! Rennie!" he says, his grip so hard on my arm I feel it all the way up to my shoulder and down to my wrist.

"You're all right. I won't let him hurt you."

He's looking straight into my eyes. "You're safe now, Rennie," he says softly, his eyes brimming with tears.

Rennie, Rennie, Rennie, Rennie, Rennie . . . echoes in my head, a chant, like a drum beat from some ancient time.

Tyler runs up, shoving at the hunk of a man. I watch as if it were far away, on some old time tiny television screen, the picture small and blurred. The man shoves Tyler's arm behind his back, pushing upward. Tyler cries out in pain.

"I'm taking you to the police station," the man says. His voice sounding distant, bubbly and water logged, barely understandable. But louder and clearer in my head rings RENNIE, RENNIE, RENNIE . . .

"Hurt her and I'll kill you!" Tyler yells.

"Hey! I'm not the guy who's hurting her! You're the one who grabbed onto her and wouldn't let her go!"

RENNIE, RENNIE . . . bouncing around in my head, in my heart, until . . .

I look at his face, look into his eyes, hear the reassurance, ". . . safe now, Rennie." Something resounds within me.

"Jack? . . . " I am shaking from head to toe.

He releases Tyler and turns to me.

"Yes," he says. "Yes."

He stands, still as a statue, his eyes on mine, moist and searching. I know he is telling the truth. He is familiar to me, not from this life, but from some other life.

"It's me, Rennie, Daddy Jack."

He takes a step toward me, his arms open. I back away. He stops, drops his arms to his side. We stand, eyes locked on one another.

"I've wanted for so long to see you again," he says.

Tyler stands rubbing his arm, watching us.

"You know this guy?" Tyler asks.

"My father," I tell him, my voice sounding whispery and unsure.

"You know *him*?" Jack asks, nodding in Tyler's direction.

"He used to be my boyfriend."

"God, Lauren . . ." Tyler starts.

"Is he bothering you?" my father says, looking at Tyler as if he could tear him apart.

"I just don't want to talk to him," I say, not meeting Tyler's eyes.

"Give me a chance, please," Tyler says, his voice shaky with emotion.

"I don't want to talk to you!"

Tyler looks from me to Jack and back again.

"Whatever," he says, and walks slowly to his car.

The promise ring shines in the sun as he rubs at a skinned place on his forehead. I look away.

Jack and I stand close, not talking. I look for something of me in him. His hair. His eyes. His lips. He reaches up and touches my hair.

"On you it looks good," he says.

A mail carrier walks by and looks curiously at the Honda parked halfway up on the sidewalk. He gives us a funny look, then walks on.

"Let's go somewhere and talk. Do you drink coffee, Rennie?" he asks.

His voice is deep and resonant, making music of my long-forgotten nickname.

"I only drink cappucino," I tell him.

"Well, let's go find one."

He opens the passenger door for me, and I get into his car.

He walks to the other side and squeezes into the Honda behind the steering wheel. He's way too big for this car.

As if he's read my mind, he laughs.

"It's the best I can do when I'm making an honest living."

Then, suddenly, he turns serious.

"That's the only kind of living I'm ever going to make again, Rennie. I'm through with all that other stuff."

I remember how Marcia swore she was through with drugs, too. But she wasn't. Only death could stop *her* drug use. I don't trust any promises about drugs.

20

I call Grams from Stark's Coffee, so she won't worry. I don't tell her who I'm with because it's way too complicated to talk about on the phone.

"A Dr. Ogden from the school called," she says. "Are you all right?"

"Fine. I'll tell you all about it when I get home."

"I hope so," she says. "I don't like the silence that's been between us the past few days. It worries me."

"I'm trying to make sense of things, Grams. That's all."

"Well . . . I love you. I'll see you in an hour or so?"

"Sure."

Jack and I sit across from one another in a corner booth, sipping our drinks. He has a double shot espresso and I have my cappucino. Two chocolate/raisin bagels sit on a plate in the middle of the table. Even though the past few hours have been wild, fighting with Shawna, seeing Tyler, I feel almost calm, sitting across from Jack.

"This is my only drug now," he says, tapping on his cup, then lifting it for a long swallow.

"I've prayed for you every day of your life, no matter how strung out I was."

Sweet, I guess. But a girl needs a lot more than prayers from her father.

"When I left you in that car in the church parking lot, with your grandmother's name and address pinned to your shirt, I told myself I'd come for you in a month, when I was clean."

He takes another long drink of coffee, then continues.

"Once, when you were seven, I was clean for two months. I wrote a letter to Frances, saying I wanted to come for you."

"You did? She didn't tell me."

"I didn't mail it. I read it over and over again, and I saw how little I had to offer you, and how uncertain my sobriety was, and I tore the letter up. I told myself if I could last six months, then maybe I'd have earned the right to see you again. But in six months I was back in jail."

He shakes his head sadly. "I've wasted so much of my life."

He looks up at me, a faint smile on his lips.

"Every birthday I've bought you a card. I've always loved you. Always."

Anger grows within me.

"Love? You think buying some kiddie birthday card means you loved me? If you loved me, you'd have quit drugs!"

The rage at Marcia, Shawna, Tyler, comes spewing out.

"Where were you when my *so-called* mother was pregnant, pumping her body and mine full of crack, or speed, or who knows what — getting me addicted before I was even born! I bet you were right there with her, smoking it or shooting up or whatever it was you were doing! You call that love?"

"Rennie . . . "

The name that was so pleasing to me a few minutes ago, grates on me now.

"Your mother, she loved you too, in her way," he says.

"Yeah! Sure! You both loved me so much I was all undernourished and full of lice when I got to Grams' house."

Jack takes a deep breath.

"We were going to quit after we made the last batch of crystal meth. We just needed a stake. I know, I know, it all sounds ridiculous now, but we were working on getting out of there, getting you out of there."

"RIGHT! AND YOU COULDN'T BOTHER TO FEED ME IN THE MEANTIME!"

People turn to look, then turn away. I don't care.

Jack gets up and comes over to my side of the booth and slides in beside me. Our shoulders are touching. I move closer to the wall, putting space between us.

"I don't blame you, Rennie. I . . . we always had cereal for you, and bananas usually. It's just . . . "

Jack takes a deep sigh and closes his eyes.

"We didn't have much room in the refrigerator for food — all the ingredients in there for meth . . . "

"How disgusting," I say, not even looking at him.

I rub my hand again, feeling the warmth from where my palm connected with Shawna's cheek.

"All I want is for us to know each other. I can't change the past, but I'd like to start now getting to know you. Showing I love you."

I'm quiet for a while, thinking. Then I tell him how the only person in the world who's ever really loved me is Grams.

"She didn't just say prayers and buy birthday cards. She got the lice out of my hair, and fed me, and took care of me when I was sick. She gave me a safe place to live. I don't even remember *anything* about Marcia. I don't even want to remember Marcia. I only remembered *you* 'cause you called me Rennie and I couldn't help it. Why *should* I remember either one of you when you couldn't ever bother to take care of me?"

"Because we're your parents. Like it or not, we're part of you."

"You make me want to puke!" I tell him.

"You seemed nicer from a distance," he says.

I push at him, wanting to get out of the booth, to get away. He sits there, like a mountain. I know how it looks, an older black man with a teenaged girl cornered in a booth. A girl who appears to be white. There's already a complaint related to his car. He has a record.

"I could yell for help. You'd be in way big trouble."

"You could," he says, all calm. "I hope we can talk for a while, but if you want to yell for help, go ahead. I've been in big trouble before — you ever been in big trouble?"

"Not really," I say, remembering the smack of Shawna's cheek beneath my hand.

After a long silence, Jack starts talking, not looking at me, like he's talking to the bagels that still sit uneaten in the middle of the table.

"It was no life for a child, we both knew that. And we'd talk, a thousand miles a minute like people do when they're on speed, about how we were going to make things better for you — get a house, white picket fence, all that American dream crap. And then we'd come down, and all we could think about was the next hit. In those brief times when I wasn't so high I was spinning, or so low I was desperate, I'd see you, clutching your filthy, friendly blanket, watching silently out of those wide, wary eyes, and I would think 'God help us. What will become of this child?' And I'd pick you up, and hold you, and make promises I couldn't keep."

"You knew Grams'd take care of me. Why didn't you send me back to her?"

"We talked about it, but we always thought we'd do better the next day. High, the world was ours. Low, we were too low to move."

"Why did you even *want* to keep me there?"

Jack lets out a long sigh and turns to face me.

"This sounds ridiculous, but addicts are ridiculous. I guess we thought we could be normal with you — you know, Mommy, Daddy, and the beautiful child."

"What a joke! I saw what I looked like when I left Texas. I was far from beautiful!"

"Addicts don't worry much about buying groceries."

"I guess addicts aren't big on personal hygiene, either," I say, all sarcastic.

"Look, Rennie. I know it was awful. If I could make it up to you, believe me, I would." he says, now looking back at the bagels.

"Tell me about the explosion," I say.

Closing his eyes and leaning his head back against the top of the booth, he talks softly, almost in a whisper.

"It was one of those god-awful hot, dry, west Texas days. Marcia and Gino were in the kitchen, doing the 'lab' work. Paul and Rex were arranging funnels and containers for the next step. The others were hanging around in the living room, in various degrees of highs and lows, watching 'I Love Lucy.' According to Craig, one of the TV watchers, you were in the doorway, between the kitchen and the living room, when it blew. I was in the driveway, unloading stuff from the car, and I swear, the ground shook like it was an earthquake. I knew right away, though, it was no earthquake.

"I grabbed a tarp from the back of the car and rushed into the house, bumping into Craig and the others rushing out. I screamed for Marcia, and for you, and from somewhere in the dense smoke, I heard your cry.

"I held the tarp in front of me and pushed through the smoke, the air growing hotter with every step I took. I was high enough not to be scared, not too high to know what I was doing. Finally I saw you and Marcia. She was holding you, trying to shield you from the smoke and fire. 'Take her,' she screamed, pushing you toward me. I took you and reached for Marcia's hand but she pulled away. 'Get her out!' she yelled.

"I was close enough to see that her whole left side was bare, clothes blown away, face, shoulder, arm, leg, all were raw and bleeding. "Go! Now!" she ordered in a voice stronger than I'd ever heard come from her. I threw the tarp over you and ran, low, trying to get under the smoke, out the door and into the yard. You were screaming and shaking. 'You're safe now, Rennie' I said to you, and you looked at me like you knew it was true. I grabbed the tarp and ran back toward the house. Before I could get there the whole thing went up. The roof, the walls — blasted to smithereens. Debris flying everywhere, then settling, leaving the most startling quiet, like the end of the world."

Jack has not moved since he began telling of the explosion. His face is without expression. His voice a monotone.

"I went kicking through debris, looking for Marcia, not caring about the others . . . "

Jack opens his eyes and turns facing me, looking intently at me, searching my face. I look away.

"Not much was left of her," he says, closing his eyes again.

"The silence was broken by voices in the distance, and sirens. Lots of them. I ran to you. You were standing exactly as I'd left you. I picked you up and started running. 'Blanket,' you whimpered once. 'Gone,' I told you, and you seemed to understand the scope of my answer, because you asked no more questions.

"You know the rest, I guess. I'd been to some Narcotics Anonymous meetings at the downtown church, when I was trying to kick it. I knew there were good people there. I left you in the unlocked car. I could tell from the stuff in the car that it belonged to a family. There was a beat-up teddy bear, and one of those juice box things with a straw in it.

"After I left you I went to the bus stop where I could watch, half out of sight. You'd only been there about ten minutes when they came. The husband and wife, and a little girl about three years old. I watched their surprise when they found you sitting in the car. Even from the distance of the bus stop, I could see that they were treating you gently. The woman helped you from the car. She seemed to be reassuring you. I watched as they walked with you back to the church office. I watched when, about thirty minutes later, the Amarillo police car drove up and two cops, a man and a woman, got out. Later, I watched as they drove away with you in the car, and as the ones who'd found you walked back to their own car, holding their daughter's hands as she swung between them.

"We could have had that, I thought, me and Marcia, with you swinging happily between us. I put my head clear down on my knees and I cried my guts out. I cried for all that would never be. I cried for your mother's broken and burned body. I cried for you, lonely in a police station. I cried for my wasted life. But a black man can't sit crying on an Amarillo bus bench for long without raising suspicion. When a squad car slowed to a near stop at the bench and then drove away, I knew it was time for me to leave. I walked and walked, then finally found a dark place under a bridge where I curled up for the night. I determined never to let drugs run my life again.

"By six the next morning I was looking for a hit."

21

W e are sitting out on the deck, in the faded canvas director's chairs, when I hear Grams pull into the driveway. She rushes through the back gate, grabbing the hoe that always leans against the back fence.

"Hello, Frances," Jack says, standing to greet her.

She stops, frozen in place.

"Jack? Jack Dillard?"

Grams looks from me to Jack and back again, confusion written on her forehead. She stands, immobile, still gripping the hoe, as if ready to use it as a weapon.

"The red Honda . . . "

"It's his," I tell her, nodding in Jack's direction.

Slowly, she lowers the hoe, then sinks into the chair across from me.

"I thought . . . I thought . . . Thank God you're all right."

I can see her hands trembling, and suddenly I realize how it must have looked to her, driving up to our house and seeing the red Honda parked there.

"It's okay, Grams," I tell her.

She looks up at Jack, who is still standing, watching.

"So much I don't understand these days . . . you here, the Honda, Lauren's sudden change of personality . . ."

"I'm sorry if my car frightened you," Jack says.

"It's just . . . we . . . someone has been stalking Lauren. And the car out front . . . "

"I wasn't stalking Lauren," Jack says. "I only wanted to see her. But I was afraid to make myself known. From a distance I could imagine that we'd get to know each other again."

"You scared us," Grams says.

"I didn't think anyone noticed me."

"We filed a complaint," Grams says.

For a fleeting moment Jack's face registers something that looks like fear. Then, in an instant, the calm returns.

Grams gets up and walks over to the African daisies at the edge of the deck. She bends down and begins pinching dead flowers off the plants. Jack sits back down in the director's chair. No one speaks. In the long silence, my thoughts are drawn back to the fight with Shawna. I've never hit a person like that before, only pretended, with the volleyball. I feel funny inside. But Tyler! Tyler and Shawna! My thoughts move on to betrayal and emptiness. On to the image of Tyler and Shawna on that awful night. Another image creeps in, though. It is Tyler fighting against Jack, taking on a man twice his size in an effort to protect me.

Back and forth the contrasting images of Tyler compete with one another, until finally Grams leaves the African daisies and stands close in front of Jack, scowling down on him.

"What do you want with us, Jack Dillard?"

"All I want is a chance to get to know my daughter."

Grams looks from Jack to me, then sits back down in the chair across from me.

"You have no custody rights. Your name's not even on her birth certificate."

"I'm talking about visiting now and then, that's all."

"She's got enough trouble right now, she doesn't need you, with your drug habit and your sleazy past."

Grams keeps talking louder and louder, faster and faster. "What do you want with her anyway? Don't think you're taking her back to Texas!"

"I just . . ."

"You and Marcia! What an awful, selfish, stupid thing you did, taking this child from me and neglecting her to the point where her very health was in danger!"

Grams is red-in-the-face mad, something I've never seen before.

"You're right. I don't want to argue with you about the past, but I *will* remind you that *I* wasn't the one who took Lauren."

"You knew it was the wrong thing for that little girl! You could have stopped it."

It's as if I'm not even here, the way they're talking about me. Sitting at the coffee place with Jack, hearing his story and the story of the explosion, I was enthralled, thinking of nothing else. Now, the Tyler emptiness is back with me, distancing me from the reality before me. I'm barely interested in their conversation, hearing it as if it were about a stranger instead of about me.

"I only want to get acquainted, Frances. I know even that's more than I deserve, but I've been clean now for over three years. I've got a decent job and I'm involved in a program to try to help kids avoid the mistakes I made."

Grams goes to the side door of the garage and brings back a large pitcher full of bird seed. She begins filling the bird feeders, first the ones outside my window, then the one hanging from the lowest branch of the walnut tree. She refills the pitcher, then takes care of the feeders hanging suspended from an iron pole at the back of the yard. Jack and I sit in our chairs, watching. The squirrels sit on two high branches, also watching. The squirrels get at least as much seed from the feeders as the birds do.

Grams returns to her chair and starts talking, as if the long pause in conversation was perfectly natural.

"I don't trust you, Jack."

"I'm not asking you to. But if I'd wanted to kidnap Lauren, I had every opportunity this afternoon. And we're sitting right here, with you."

Grams nods. "I suppose you've got a point," she says.

"If I could just visit with Lauren once a week or so. You know, stop by with some sodas and chips or something and just sit and talk. I'd only come over when you're here, if you'd feel better about that."

"I don't know," Grams says.

Although I've not been paying close attention to the conversation, I notice no one is considering what *I* might want.

"Does anyone want *my* opinion?"

They both look at me, startled.

"You *are* talking about me, aren't you?"

"I guess you're right," Grams says. "What *is* your opinion?"

"Well, I'd like to get acquainted, too," I say.

I glance over at Jack and see tears welling in his eyes.

"All right, then," Grams says. "You're nearly grown up now, anyway. It should be your decision. But I want it the way Jack said, short visits here, in my presence."

"Fine," I say.

Grams wants to hear about the explosion. Jack tells her the story in the same manner as he told me — head back, eyes closed, monotone voice. Grams, too, closes her eyes as she listens, unmoving except for an occasional shiver. I listen to the whole thing again, too, vividly imagining the scene, seeing it as Jack describes, mixing it with dream images, wondering if memory is creeping back.

"At least she did something good at the end," Grams says, her cheeks wet with tears.

"She wasn't all bad," Jack says.

"God damned drugs," Grams says.

Jack pulls his chair closer to Grams.

"Nothing I can say can express how grateful I am to you,

Frances. I see what a wonderful young woman Lauren's become, and I know it's because of the security and love you've offered her. I'd give anything if I could go back and be the kind of father I should have been, but that's useless talk."

"Being able to raise Lauren is one of the greatest gifts of my life," Grams tells him. "I wish it had happened under other circumstances, but getting Lauren gave me new meaning. What a wonder she is," Grams says.

Grams' love is so kind, and so strong, it seems I should be happy with that. But my loss of Tyler keeps dragging me down.

Twice while Jack is there, the phone rings and it is Tyler. Jack watches as I let the call go unanswered. "Please talk to me," is always the message, and I always erase it immediately.

"I know it's too soon for me to be giving fatherly advice, but I think you ought to hear the guy out," he says to me as he's getting ready to leave.

"You don't know what he's done," I say.

"I know one thing he's done. He tried to protect *you* today. And, as far as *he* knew, he was putting his own life at risk in the process. That's no small thing."

"The other thing he did was no small thing, either."

"Well, you maybe ought to hear his side. You heard my side and it made a little difference, didn't it?"

I nod my head.

"Well, then, at least think about it," he says, standing to leave.

He looks from me to Grams and back again.

"Keep calling me Jack, if you like, because that's how you know me. But when I finally decided to put my drug life behind me, I went back to Jacob, the name my parents gave me."

Before he walks out the gate, Jack, Jacob, opens his arms to me. This time, I let him hug me. "Rennie, Rennie, Rennie," he whispers.

As mad as I've been at him for most of my life, I sense a connection, some mysterious father-daughter thing.

I walk to the driveway and watch the little red Honda drive down the street, and I think about how different it seems now than it did yesterday, when seeing the same car cast fear in my heart.

For a little while I feel at ease within myself, but then I think of Tyler. And Shawna. And betrayal and emptiness again fill my soul.

22

It is after sixth period, in The Harp's office. I've stayed away from creative writing for more than two weeks now, and can't imagine how I'll ever go back.

"This is not an independent studies class you know, Lauren. We need your participation."

"But I've been doing my work. The 'Habitat for Humanity' article is ready to go, and my 'You Don't Know Me Unless You Know . . .' piece is finished."

Mr. Harper shakes his head sadly. "There's a lot more to writing than writing," he says.

I think that's a dumb thing to say, but I wait for what's next.

"Especially in journalism. If you're going to be a journalist you'll be involved in editorial meetings and decisions, and in collaboration with editors for revision. It's not just you."

"Can't you give me a little more time? Let me work on my own for another week or so?"

"Look, I know a little bit about what happened. Not the details, but the general idea. And I don't think I'm betraying any confidence when I say that Tyler has told me you won't even talk to him."

Harper turns his attention back to a tall stack of papers on his desk and picks up his red pen.

"I need you to level with me, Lauren. I can't give you another week out of class unless there's a compelling reason to do that. You may *have* a compelling reason, but I sure as hell don't know what it is."

We're on the second floor. From where I'm sitting I can see kids milling around, waiting for the late bus. Some are weighed down with backpacks so heavy they'll likely end up with back trouble for life. The burly security guy is out there, joking around with some gang wannabees. The huge oak tree is only bare branches now, leafless and exposed. That's how I feel, bare, skeletal, unmasked.

Harp reads through a paper, jotting comments in the margin. Then he sets it on top of a shorter stack of papers. He watches me for a moment. I don't know how to explain to Harper that walking into the classroom, seeing Tyler in his front row desk, seeing Blake, and all the rest, would be like walking in without my skin, all of my precious, fragile organs exposed to harsh elements.

"I've got time," Harper says, picking up another paper from the taller stack and working through it with his red remarks.

When he finishes that paper he tells me, "I know this sounds trite, and like some old guy who doesn't understand, but everyone loses a love. It doesn't mean you have to lose yourself in the process."

I fight back tears. How can anyone possibly understand how I feel? And what good would it do if they did?

"Come to class tomorrow," Harper says as he picks up the next paper.

"Can't I wait until Monday?"

"Not unless you want your grade lowered by one letter. We need you on the editorial board. We need you on the ads committee. You're not the only one who's hurting, you know? Alcoholic parents, a dad with terminal cancer, poverty, pregnancy, you can find it all in creative writing. Take a lesson from your classmates. Gather your courage and get on with your life."

I grab my backpack and charge out the door, slamming it hard behind me. I never knew Harper could be so cold, like he doesn't even care! I rush to the gym where I find Amber by her locker, already dressed for practice. I spew out my anger with Harper, how he won't even let me wait until Monday to start back to class, how he doesn't even *try* to understand, how I know he likes Tyler better, anyway. I expect Amber to be on my side, to agree that Harper is being totally unfair with me.

She gives me a long look.

"I'll see you on the court," is all she says, then sprints off to practice.

I jerk my locker open and strip down, grab my volleyball shirt and shorts, change shoes and jam my clothes into the locker. I slam the door hard enough to hear the rattle, then go out to the courts. I'm the last one there. Coach Terry says, "See me after practice, please, Lauren."

God! I wish people would get off my back. Like I don't have enough trouble as it is!

I serve the ball, open handed, sending a satisfying sting through my hand, up my arm and straight into my head. I think of Marcia, the Marcia mash, but when the ball comes to me I'm gentle with it, using only my fingertips to get it over to Amber, setting her up for a spike. The ball is back to me again. "Marcia," I think, and fail to return it.

"Time out," Coach Terry calls, then runs over to me. "You okay?"

"Fine," I tell her, which is way far from the truth, but I don't think she's asking for my life story.

"Sit out a bit," she says, calling one of the sophomore girls in to take my place.

On the bench I think "Marcia, Marcia," trying to get the old fire back, trying to feel the heat of anger. Instead I feel the heat of fire, of her pushing me toward Jack, demanding that he save me and leave her behind. All of these years of anger — I can't quite get a grip on that anymore.

I'm more angry with Harp than I've ever been, but it's not a kind of slam-the-volleyball anger, picturing his face shattering. Too much. I watch the play, wondering where Amber gets *her* power.

Coach calls me back in for the last five minutes of play, but something is lost from my game. I can't slam Marcia. I can't slam Shawna because it was too awful the time I did it for real.

When I go to Coach's office, she has me sit in the standard place, on the "visitor" side of her desk. She sits in one of those big easy-on-your-back kind of reclining chairs.

"What's up with you, Lauren?"

I shrug my shoulders.

"You sick?"

"Not really," I say.

"Well?"

"I don't know," I lie.

"Love problems I suppose. I haven't noticed Tyler sniffing around lately."

Why can't teachers mind their own business?

Coach Terry waits for me to talk, but, same as with Harper — what can I say? I'm lost? I'm betrayed? My soul has shrunk to the size of a raisin, and I can't even find it anymore? Life has lost all meaning? And if I said any of these things would I be whisked off to some school counselor who'd never ever been in love but would know it all anyway? Better to stay silent.

"Well, whatever your problem, let's hope you get your game back," Coach Terry says.

I take this for my cue to leave. Amber is waiting for me by my locker. I change and we walk out together.

"Wanna go to Barb 'n Edie's?" she asks.

"I don't think so," I say.

"Well, I do," she says. "I think I'll go back and see if Candy wants to go with me. Talk to you later."

Before I even know what's happening, Amber's disappeared back inside the gym building. Well, all right. Let her find Candy. Why should I care?

I told Grams I'd take the bus today, since she had to work this morning and then had a bunch of errands to do. But when I get near the bus stop and see the crowd of kids, I decide to walk. I've only gone a few blocks when Jack pulls up beside me and rolls down the window.

"Rennie. I was hoping I'd see you. Want a ride?"

"Sure," I say, and get into the once fearsome red Honda.

"My three o'clock appointment didn't show, so I've got about an hour to bum around. Do you want coffee?"

"Well . . . "

"I called Frances to see if she'd mind if I took you to Stark's. She didn't have a problem with it."

"Okay then," I say.

We order the exact same thing we had that first day. This time we sit at a table outside, though.

"Those people in the east where the snow is so high they can't even go to work don't know what they're missing," Jack laughs.

He turns his face upward, eyes closed, and basks in the warmth of the sun like some kind of lizard, or maybe a cat.

"Thank you, Lord," he whispers, then turns to me, smiling his gentle, contented smile.

"Are you religious?" I ask him.

"Not exactly," he says. "But a higher power helped me get clean and helps me stay clean. I can't do it by myself."

"Like God?" I ask.

"Well, I guess so. I usually just think higher power, or HP for short. Lots of people think God, though."

"How did God, or whatever, help you get clean?"

"I don't know. It's a mystery. But since I've been working this program, and paying attention to HP, I like to express my thanks for life. Like for this sunny day, and for you. For the trees and the mountains . . . "

"I don't believe in God," I tell him.

"What do you believe in?"

"I don't know," I say, taking a gulp of cappucino, trying to swallow my tears. "I used to believe in me and Tyler, but not anymore."

"Tyler. The guy who was trying to save you? The guy who keeps wanting to talk to you?"

I nod.

"If you don't believe in this Tyler guy anymore, then what?"

"I guess Grams is the only one left who I know will be there for me."

"Too soon to tell, for me, huh?"

"Way too soon," I say.

"How about space aliens?"

"Nah . . . Maybe . . . I don't know."

"How about the overall goodness of humankind?"

"Right," I say, all sarcastic. "Did *you* watch the news last night? Those three guys who killed a homeless guy because he asked them for a dollar?"

Jack takes a bite out of the bagel and chews carefully, watching me all the while.

"Sorry if I sound cynical," I say. "I've been having sort of a hard time lately."

"I gathered. Have you decided to hear his side of things yet?"

"No," I say, feeling my muscles tense in resistance. What business is it of Jack's anyway?

A big bluejay lands on the sidewalk near our table and starts pecking at crumbs. Jack tosses a bite of bagel down to it. It eats fast and starts squawking. Jack laughs.

"I like jays," Jack says. "They know exactly what they want. . . . Do you, Lauren? Do you know what you want?"

I shake my head.

Between questions from Harp and Coach Terry this afternoon, and now Jack, it seems like I'm on some kind of witness stand. I'm tired of it.

As if he's sensed my mood, Jack says, "I don't mean to be nosy. It's just that I've missed out on so many years with you, I'm in a hurry to get caught up. Just tell me to jump back if I'm asking too much."

Jack throws another handful of crumbs down near the jay. Another one comes swooping in to get in on the feast, but the first jay is not big on sharing. We sit watching the birds for a while, then Jack looks at his watch.

"Come on, I'll take you home. I've got an appointment to show a couple of newlyweds a condominium. Can't keep 'em waiting."

On the way home Jack asks me about the blonde he always was seeing me with.

"She's with another friend today," I say.

He takes his eyes off the road long enough to check out my expression.

"Isn't that okay?" he says.

"Whatever," I say. "She acted sort of mad."

"So, who all's mad at you right now — or the other way around. Who all are you mad at?"

"Well, Tyler. And Shawna. Mr. Harper, my creative writing teacher, and Coach Terry, my volleyball coach."

"You mad at your gramma?"

"No."

"Me?"

"Not right now."

"Oh, but you're *going* to get mad at me any minute now?"

"No. It's just . . . I used to be mad at you for a long time."

"But no more?"

"Maybe not. I'm not sure."

"But you're giving me a chance, right?"

I nod.

"That's all I ask," he tells me, "just a chance."

He pulls into the driveway at Grams' and lets me out, then leaves for his appointment. No sooner have I put my backpack down when I hear another car. It is Amber. I open the back door for her and she stomps past me into the kitchen. I follow her. She abruptly turns and faces me.

"I thought I could trust you!"

"What do you mean?"

"Don't act all innocent! You promised you wouldn't tell anyone and I believed you!"

She is crying now, red in the face, fists clenched.

"Probably the whole school knows I've got herpes because of your big fat mouth!"

"What . . . ?"

And then I get it. Tyler must have told . . . Oh, God. It feels as if someone has slammed me over the head with a baseball bat. I step backward, barely breathing.

"Amber . . . "

"Blake took me home from Barb 'n Edie's. We're laughing and talking and then he gets all serious. 'I love you so much, herpes couldn't turn me off,' he says. I can't *believe* you'd tell Blake that I had herpes. I trusted you!"

"I didn't tell Blake," I say.

"Well, someone did and you're the only other person who knows! Who *knew*!"

Amber sinks down into a chair and puts her head down on the kitchen table — the same table where we worked on Brownie projects together, and struggled over algebra, and where Grams told us both about menstruation when Amber asked, after her mother had refused to talk about the subject — the table we sat at when we made tiny pin pricks of blood and held our wrists together, vowing we'd be sister-friends for life.

She is shaking with sobs.

"Oh, God, Amber. I'm so sorry. Damn Tyler!"

"It's not Tyler! It's *YOU*! You broke your promise to me. You took my most private secret and spread it around!"

"I didn't spread it around! Tyler promised he wouldn't tell! I didn't plan to tell him, it's just, we were arguing, you know, about my virginity plan, and it sort of slipped out."

"And then it slipped out to Blake and who knows where it's slipping right now! I'm so embarrassed . . . and if my mom finds out . . . "

I thought I already felt as bad as I possibly could, what with the loss of Tyler and all we had been to one another. But I feel even worse now. Why *had* I told Tyler about Amber? I'd give anything if I could take it back. But watching Amber, seeing the hurt in her eyes, I know there's no taking it back now. I'm filled with guilt.

"Could we just decide we're not blood sisters anymore?" Amber says.

It's like someone has kicked me in the stomach — knocked the breath right out of me. I sit across the table from her, wishing I could make things better.

"I made a terrible mistake," I tell her. "I'm so sorry."

I reach for Amber's hand. She draws it away from me, like I'm fire.

"You're not my blood sister," she says. "Blood sisters don't tell each others' secrets."

She stands and walks out the door. I follow.

"But we *are* blood sisters," I say. "We can't change that."

"You changed it when you broke your promise to me."

Amber walks away, faster. I catch up with her.

"I'm *sorry*! I'll never do anything like that again. Give me a chance! Think about how I've always been there for you!"

She turns and gives me such a look . . .

"I *have* always been there for you."

"In your dreams," she says.

I can tell by the way she's breathing, slow and deliberate, that she's trying hard not to cry again.

"Your blabbing my secret is only the final blow," she says.

"I don't even know what you mean," I tell her.

"My point exactly! It's like you're the only person in the world with a problem. Half the time when I call you, you can't be bothered to call back. And then when I see you at school you just shrug it off — 'I was feeling too down to call,' you say."

Her face is red again, and her voice is up about an octave.

"What if *I'm* feeling down? Who do *I* talk to? My mom doesn't want me going out with Blake — she's decided he's the Antichrist or something and it turns out you were right, I like him, and who can I tell any of that stuff to? No one knows me as well as you do, but you're out there on Pluto or a mile underground, or somewhere that you can't be reached."

Her lower lip is quivering.

"I'm sorry," I say. "I didn't know."

"How could you know when you don't listen and you don't ask?"

Her deep blue eyes are all watery again, and tears are sliding down her cheeks. She is so pretty, and so nice, how could I have forgotten how lucky I was to have her for my best, best friend. How could I have told her secret?

She turns and starts walking again.

"No! Don't leave. Please. I'm sorry. Give me a chance," I beg. "I want us always to be sister-friends. I want always to be there for you. Tell me about your mom."

"Why, so you can go blab my business to someone else?"

I am so ashamed, there is nothing more to say. Amber gets in her car and drives away. I wander out to the deck and sit thinking of all Amber and I have been through together, our years of being best friends, and I can't believe I've ruined it. When the phone rings I go to the door to hear if there's a message. It's Tyler. This time I pick up.

"How *could* you have told Blake about Amber having herpes?"

"I didn't tell Blake," Tyler says.

"I don't believe you."

"Don't then, but I didn't tell Blake. I wouldn't do that."

"Who did you tell then?"

"I didn't tell anyone. I promised you I wouldn't tell and I swear I didn't. But Lauren, I want to talk about . . . "

"Why should I believe you?"

"Well, for starters, because I've never lied to you."

"Well then, how did Blake know?"

"I don't know. But I've got to see you. We've got to talk, and not about Blake and Amber, either. We've got to talk about you and me."

"No," I say, but I'm not sure I mean it anymore.

I'm so confused about everything. My whole world is upside down — the loss of Tyler. Jack's re-entry into my life. The new knowledge that *both* my parents, not just Jack, saved me from a fiery death. The loss of Amber's friendship. It's all too much to deal with, and I don't know what to do or where to turn.

"I've got to go now," I tell Tyler.

"I didn't tell Blake, or anyone, about Amber, and I did what I did with Shawna partly for you."

I hang up, then dial Amber's number.

"Tyler swears he didn't tell a soul," I say.

Amber sounds hysterical, half laughing, half crying.

"What is it? Talk to me, Amber!"

She gasps out that it was all a misunderstanding.

"Blake called about fifteen minutes ago, wanting to know why I got out of the car right when he was telling me how much he loved me. 'All I could think of was the herpes business,' I told him. He goes 'you didn't even give me a chance to finish — herpes wouldn't turn me off, or AIDS, or syphilis, or pimples all over your pretty face, or rotting teeth . . . "

"What?"

"He was trying to tell me how much he loved me, that nothing would turn him off," Amber says. "I totally jumped to conclusions."

"So Tyler really didn't tell him?"

"No. I just thought . . . I'm so relieved . . ."

I want to turn cartwheels and dance under the stars.

"*I'm* so relieved," I tell her.

"It doesn't change the fact that you broke your promise to me, though."

"But . . . could you give me another chance? Can't we still be blood sisters?"

"I don't know," she says, and hangs up.

23

I get to Amber's before seven in the morning. Mrs. Brody, in the yellow chenille bathrobe she's had ever since I've known her, answers the door.

"Come in, Lauren. Have you had breakfast? How about a scrambled egg?"

She's always like that — offering food before I even get into the house.

"Maybe an orange?" I say, nodding toward the fruit bowl. It's not that I want an orange, but I know she won't relax until she sees me eating something.

Mrs. Brody cuts the orange into sections, puts it on a small glass plate, and hands it to me.

"How's your grandmother?" she asks.

"Fine," I say. "Is Amber up?"

"She'd better be. Why don't you go see?"

I go down the hall to Amber's room, where she's sitting on her bed, putting on her shoes. She gives me this big, wide grin, which fades immediately. Like she suddenly remembers she's mad.

"What's up?" she says, all cold and distant.

"Helium balloons," I say, but she doesn't laugh.

"I want to ask you, really seriously, to give me another chance. That's all."

"I'll think about it," Amber says in a whisper.

"Do you want a ride to school?"

She shakes her head.

"Well . . . see you in peer communications," I say.

I walk out to the kitchen, put the orange peels in the disposal, the dish in the dishwasher, and go on to school.

Even though I sit right behind Amber in peer communications, it's as if we're strangers. At lunchtime I sit in my car by myself and read *Jane Eyre*. I'm not hungry.

At volleyball practice Amber and I set each other up, working together as we always do. Volleyball's the same, except for laughter and words of encouragement, and our special handshake that lines up the blood sister spots on our wrists.

Big exceptions.

It is not until I've showered and dressed that Amber breaks the silence between us.

"I've been thinking," she says.

"Me, too. A lot."

We walk together to the parking lot and stand leaning against my grams' car.

"I was so shocked that you would tell my secret," Amber says. "I know that if Blake and I keep getting closer, I'll tell him about my herpes. But I want it to come from me, not from anyone else."

I only listen. I've already apologized, and asked for another chance. What else is there to say?

Amber takes a deep breath. "Last night, my mom was looking through old photos. She's putting together this family history thing and redoing a bunch of old albums. She kept calling me to look at photos. A bunch of them were of you and me — camping, in our look-alike Halloween pumpkin costumes, one from when we first started playing volleyball, back in seventh grade. Boy, were we dorky looking."

Amber smiles and I smile back, awkward.

"There was one of us at the beach, which reminded me of how you saved my life when I got knocked down by that giant wave and you pulled me out of the water."

"I didn't save your life. You'd have gotten out on your own."

"I'd gone under for the third time."

This is an old argument. Amber was only about two feet from shore when I grabbed her arm and pulled her up to the damp sand.

"I only gave you a hand," I say.

"I was drowning."

We stand next to each other for a long time, quiet, thinking. Each of us, I suppose, remembering so many times together. Finally, I get up the nerve to ask, "Wanna go get something to drink?"

Amber nods and we get into the car. We go to a drive-thru and order sodas and fries, then sit eating them in front of Amber's house.

"I'm sorry I told Tyler," I say, as if I can't say it enough. "And I'm sorry I've been so wrapped up in my own troubles I haven't been much of a friend lately."

Amber nods and shoves a handful of fries into her mouth, like she does when she's tense.

"You said your mom doesn't like Blake," I say, hoping Amber will talk with me like we're friends again.

She finishes the rest of her french fries and I hand her mine.

"What doesn't she like about him?" I prompt.

Amber looks at me, like she can't decide whether to talk or not. But then she starts.

"Oh, you know how my mother gets — all judgmental and protective. When Blake first met her she asked him what he wanted to be when he grew up. Like she'd ask a six-year-old. He told her he was a poet. And then she went all 'rhyme something.' How embarrassing! Anyway he said he wasn't a rhyming poet, his style was more like Allen Ginsberg."

"Oh, no!"

"Not that my mom knows anything about Allen Ginsberg, but she knows he's in league with the devil."

With that we both laugh, thinking of gentle Blake in league with the devil. We laugh and laugh until we're worn out with laughter and the barriers between us have weakened.

"See, if I were to tell Candy that my mom thought Blake was in league with the devil, she wouldn't have a clue, I'd have to explain all about my mom, and her church . . . but you, you get the whole picture right away."

"Years of knowing you and your mom . . . "

"I like Blake, a lot. It's hard though, because we want to see each other, and I don't want to lie to my mom. But I think she's being completely unreasonable to tell me I can't go out with him."

"She'd like him if she'd get to know him," I say.

"Yeah. She said he could come for dinner Sunday. That seems so phony to me, but it might help."

After we've tried to figure out ways Amber can convince her mom that it's okay to go out with Blake, and talked about all that she likes about him, the conversation shifts, and I try to catch Amber up on what's been going on with me. It's not that everything is exactly okay between us, but that things are *starting* to get better.

I go through the whole story about Tyler and Shawna again, and how it's as if I've been living way underwater and only hearing and seeing things from a great distance. Floating. Disconnected.

"And THEN, my father found me . . ."

"WHAT?"

"Yeah. It's so amazing. The guy in the red Honda . . . "

"The ex-addict? Jacob?"

"Yeah. Jack."

"Your father?"

I tell her the whole story, and how it was sort of mystical, when

Jack called me Rennie, like a deeply buried memory suddenly unearthed.

After a long silence Amber says, "I'm glad we're talking."

"Me, too. Thanks for giving me a chance."

Amber nods.

I take a long, deep breath and realize that my hands and feet are no longer numb, and that even though the Tyler hurt is still there, so's a lot of other stuff, like being a friend to Amber, and caring about Grams, and getting to know Jack.

We talk on and on, until sunlight fades.

"I'd better get inside to help with dinner," Amber says. "I'll see you tomorrow."

"Well . . ."

"You're not cutting school *again?*"

"I'm taking tomorrow to figure some things out, but Thursday, I'll be back, in all of my classes, for good."

"Are you still mad at Mr. Harper?"

"No. He was right, you know, about how I should gather courage and get on with my life."

"And Shawna?" she asks softly.

"Ummm. Grams has been talking to me a lot lately about how destructive it is to hold onto anger. But Shawna . . . "

Amber stands waiting for me to complete my sentence, but no more words come to me.

"You know, it really wasn't all her fault."

"I know. And she got kicked out of Hamilton High for fighting with me, when really, I'm the one who hit her. She didn't even hit back."

"I saw her at the Habitat house yesterday," Amber says. "She told me she likes it better at Sojourner. Everybody works at their own pace, and there's no in-groups or out-groups."

"You saw her?"

"Yeah. We've all been working on the landscaping at the Habitat house. Did you think everything stopped when you withdrew from life?"

I'm quiet — thinking about what she's said.

"I'm sorry. That sounded mean."

"It's just been so hard," I say, trying not to let tears come.

Amber gathers up her stuff and opens the car door.

"Bye, Sister B.," I say as she gets out of the car.

"Bye," she says, leaving silent air where I want to hear her call me Sister K.

I get up at six-thirty in the morning, put on jeans, a T-shirt, and a sweatshirt. These used to be my tightest jeans, but now I have to tighten the waist with a belt just to keep them up. It seems like a long time since I've wanted to eat anything. I could probably make a lot of money if I wrote *The No-Fail Broken Heart Diet.*

After I finish my second hot, steaming cup of tea, I put the cup in the dishwasher. I've promised Grams I'll not skip meals anymore, so I get fruit, cheese, trail mix and a bottle of water and stuff it into my backpack. I brush my teeth, then get my journal and creative writing folder, along with my favorite pen and an extra, and add those to my backpack supplies. I leave a note for Grams, telling her not to worry if the school calls about my absence. I've taken a day to get myself together. Tomorrow I'll throw myself back into school.

I'm not certain what the schedule is for the twenty-seven bus, but I know if I wait long enough it will come along. I sit on the bench at the corner of Garfield and Alameda, half-reading *Jane Eyre,* half people-watching. A youngish, tired looking woman sits beside me. She is carrying a large, cracked, vinyl shoulder bag, and a small paper sack which I take to be her lunch. She sits quietly on the bench, both bags on her lap, staring straight ahead. I notice that her hands are thick-skinned and tough looking. Maybe she cleans houses for a living. Some people have such hard lives — I'm going to try not to feel sorry for myself anymore.

I go back to reading *Jane Eyre.* She has been deceived by her love, Mr. Rochester, but she forgives him. Also, having finished reading *Angela's Ashes*, I know Frank McCourt forgives his drunken father. I think about how Grams is always telling me I've got to get past my anger at Marcia. I'm not sure I can be as forgiving as Jane Eyre or Frank McCourt. I'm not even sure I want to be. But I definitely want Amber to forgive me. Maybe everything's all related, and I have to learn about forgiving in order to be forgiven? The idea makes my head spin.

Finally, the twenty-seven bus pulls up and I and the young woman with the tough hands board it.

It is a slow trip to the foothills, stopping every two blocks to pick people up or let them off. The bus is crowded by city hall — standing room only. Then, after the welfare office, it is nearly empty again. I'm the only one left at the very last stop. As I step down off the bus, the driver, a big, burly woman with a kindly face asks, "Shouldn't you be in school today?"

"I'm off track," I tell her, as if I were on break from a year-round school. It's not exactly a lie. I've been "off track" for over two weeks now.

"Oh," she says, then closes the pneumatic doors behind me.

I start out on the trail to Clark's Peak. The friendly, fall, California sun is warm on my back and I soon peel off my sweatshirt and tie it around my waist. The scent of sage is fresh and strong, mingled in the refreshing pine-filled air. I breathe deeply, purifying my smog-wearied lungs.

At the place where we found Baby Hope I pause to recreate that scene in my mind — the nearly dead baby, gaining breath and color as Grams worked with her. Again I reflect on how uncertain life is. The "what ifs" flood through me.

I put my sweatshirt down on the ground, covering sticky pine needles. I sit crosslegged, yoga style, then get my journal and begin writing.

What if Grams and I *hadn't* happened along the trail that day four years ago? Such a simple decision on that fateful morning — should we hike Big Santa Anita Canyon, or should we stay closer to home and hike along the Clark's Peak trail? We changed countless lives in the choice of Clark's Peak. Baby Hope's of course — it *gave* her a life. And Sarah Mabry's — it meant she was convicted of attempted murder rather than actual murder.

Finding Hope turned me away from childhood toward adulthood, making me realize the importance of my actions. Maybe some of the doctors and nurses and paramedics who took care of Baby Hope were changed, too. Who knows? Then there's Hope's new family — her mom, dad, grandparents, and all the other people Hope will touch in her whole lifetime. What if she grows up to develop a cure for cancer. That *could* happen. Or, whoa! What if she grows up to be a mass murderer? And then, there would be all the people murdered, and their devastated families and friends. Or, the happy ending, all those people cured of cancer, and their relieved families and friends. All because of that one simple decision to hike this trail.

I go on to other "what ifs." Like, what if I'd not seen Tyler and Shawna together that night? Would I still be in love and happy, instead of feeling lost and empty? Is it true that what you don't know can't hurt you? I don't think so. If you're driving, and you don't know how to use the brakes . . . If I were going along right now, thinking everything was just fine with Tyler, wouldn't that be like living a lie?

An hour must have passed since I first sat down to write. My back is tired and my butt is numb. Slowly, I get to my feet and stretch. I take a large, Fuji apple from my backpack and bite into it. The crisp, sweet flavor catches me off guard, reminding me of the first time I ever tasted a Fuji apple. I remember the careful way Tyler opened his Swiss army knife, and how he cut the apple in slices, working around the core instead of quartering it. We slowly savored the taste and texture, and then, having nothing left but the core, we kissed. Our apple-fresh lips met and we kissed, really kissed, for the first time.

I pick up my backpack and walk the rest of the way to the peak, wanting to forget that kiss, wanting to forget that there will be no more kisses with Tyler.

At the peak I turn and look out over the valley. The sky is pure blue and cloudless, untainted by the usual industrial strength smog. I can see the large brick buildings on the college campus where Tyler and I used to park. To the west is a big, stone church with its steeple reaching upward. It is easy to identify the Hamilton High football stadium, where only three short weeks ago I sat with Tyler and our friends. Three weeks ago and a lifetime away.

From where I stand, I can figure out where the Habitat house is. I can't exactly see it, but I know it is there.

Further south, in the Whittier Hills, a huge Buddhist Temple casts a faint, rosy reflection. Best of all though, the sight that has always thrilled me on the rare occasions of such visibility, is the gleaming ocean, the demarcation between land and water and then, in the shimmering distance, Catalina Island. I drink in the vision. Such days come only once or twice a year, and I am lucky to be here this day, as Grams and I were lucky to have been here on that day four years ago. Sometimes life presents us with gifts, like this day of such beauty, or the opportunity to rescue the baby on the trail. And then, smack! In the dimmed light of a nursery office, life turns cruel.

I haul back and, with all my strength, throw my apple core out over the cliff. I'm glad to be the only one in the picnic area this morning. I get out my writing materials again and sit on one of the creaky wooden benches. My pen rushes to keep up with my thoughts. First there's Tyler, then Shawna, Amber, Grams, Marcia, Jack, Mr. Harper, Coach Terry, Blake. Every hurt, real and imagined, balanced by pleasures small and large. Everything I can't express out loud, the sweet thoughts and the hateful, murderous thoughts. They come without censorship. Anger, love, disappointment, jealousy, guilt, rage, hope, the innermost hidden thoughts and the silliest nonsense, all fly across the paper, page after page. When my hand gets so tired I can't write another sentence, I tear out a blank piece of notebook paper to use as a kind of placemat, and set my lunch stuff on it.

Slowly peeling the orange, I read back over everything I've written this morning. It's barely legible, I've written so fast. That's fine. I don't want anyone else to read it anyway.

I've written a lot about Amber, and how important her friendship is to me. How wrong it was of me to tell her secret, even to someone I trusted with all my heart. How wrong of me it was, too, to withdraw from everyone around me. Through all of this writing, I think I've figured out that just because I've lost Tyler, doesn't mean I have to lose everything else, too.

One of the things that shows up in my writing is the idea of giving people chances. I wrote about how Tyler kept leaving messages for me, asking me to give him a chance. And then how Jack had told me all he wanted from me was a chance. Then yesterday *I* was begging Amber to give *me* a chance. The Harp says when we notice recurring themes or events in our dreams, we need to explore below the surface. In our journals, too, if the same subject or theme keeps showing up, unbidden, it's a sign that our unconscious mind is sending us a message. Is my unconscious mind trying to tell me something about chances?

I mull these things over as I slowly eat away at the chunk of jack cheese sitting next to the peeled orange on my notebook paper. Everyone who loves me, Grams, Amber, Jack, keeps hinting, strongly, that I should listen to Tyler. But no one else can really understand how fragile and shattered I feel at the very core of my being. How can I possibly open myself up to more hurt?

Twelve Cub Scouts, in uniforms, come rushing into the picnic area. Two men, dads I guess, come dragging along behind.

"Carl! Carl! I don't want to have to tell you again — keep your hands to yourself!"

"Yeah! Carl!" says a big, pudgy kid with a belly befitting a beer drinker.

I can tell already these are scouts working on their bickering badges. I pack up and walk back down the hill. Once out of earshot of the den, I stop and look out again over the valley. The afternoon has brought a slight haze now, shielding Catalina from view. Maybe it's the beauty of the day. Maybe it's a light shed by writing. Maybe it's finally being tired of misery. Whatever. I feel peaceful. Worried and guilty about Amber. Hurt and betrayed by Tyler, all of that is still there, but that's not *all* I've got now. From a secret place within me, I feel an old strength rising. I'll work things out with Amber. I'll get past this thing with Tyler. I've decided. And I've decided to listen the next time he wants to talk.

Gather courage. Gather courage. That's what I keep telling myself as I walk toward the creative writing classroom. Yesterday, it seemed simple. I would just walk in and face everyone. Today, though, I'm not sure I can do it. My heart is pounding and my mouth is all dry. When I get to the door, instead of opening it, I turn to walk away.

"Uh, uh," Harper says, juggling his thermos in the same hand as the stacks of papers and books he always carries, and gently taking my arm with the other.

"It'll be okay," he says, standing at the door, his arms too full to open it.

Megan and Kelsey come up behind us, reach around and open the door.

"Hey, look who's back," Kelsey says, all friendly.

"It's about time," Megan says.

I can't look at them.

"Hi," I say, gazing at the floor.

Harper leads me inside, then goes to his desk and dumps his armload of stuff. I walk to the back of the room, to the far corner, and sit down. Blake comes back to talk to me.

"Hey, come sit with us. Today's group work."

I shake my head. He sits down beside me.

"If Muhammed won't come to the mountain, the mountain will come to Muhammed," he laughs.

"Blake . . . "

"No. Come on. We need you."

"Not today," I say, wishing there were a window I could jump from, anything to get away. But no, we're in the basement.

"Okay," Blake says, "but you're missing a lot."

He walks back to his seat near the front. Tyler comes in just as the bell rings and flops down in his usual place. I know he didn't notice me when he came in, but I see Blake whisper to him and then he turns to find me. For the briefest moment our eyes meet, then I look away. But I see enough to notice he looks tired, and thin, and sad.

During quick-write I don't want to write about anything I'm feeling — nervous, scared, embarrassed, being in the same classroom with Tyler, where probably *everyone* by now knows how he and Shawna have made such a fool of me. I write about the desks, the chairs, the floor, the ceiling, the lights, Mr. Harper's thermos, only inanimate things. Emotionless things.

Once I glance up to see that Tyler is tasting a seed. Blake looks all confident. It feels like a scene from years ago.

Harper doesn't call on me to participate. I sit through the whole class, my head down, gazing at the desktop, not hearing what's going on around me, waiting for the bell.

When I walk out into the hallway, Tyler is waiting for me.

"This is the last time I'm asking," he says. "Can we talk?"

I nod my head.

"Meet me at the bench after you're finished with volleyball practice."

I nod my head again, fighting tears. As he walks away, I notice that he is still wearing our promise ring. What a joke. But I'm not laughing.

Tyler is not at the bench when I get there. I sit down and pretend to be reading *Jane Eyre*. But all I can think of is Tyler. All I can feel is hurt. All I can do is try not to cry.

After ten minutes I decide he's not coming. Who cares? Just as I stand to leave, though, he comes running, top speed, around the corner of the main building. I sit back down.

He dumps his backpack on the ground and sits beside me on the bench. He tries to talk and catch his breath at the same time.

"Afraid — puff — you'd — puff, puff — be — gone."

"I thought you weren't coming," I say.

"I needed to go home after school — puff — to pick up clean overalls for work."

Tyler takes a few deep breaths, then continues.

"There was plenty of time. But then Mom insisted on keeping the car to go to the store. So I had to *literally* run back here."

Tyler pauses and gives me one of those long, intense looks.

"Listen to me, talking like it's you and me, in the old way, when there's so much else."

He is so familiar to me, the hint of fresh soil in his healthy clean scent, the tiny scar at the edge of his left eyebrow. But his face looks dark and dull — older. Tears gather in his eyes.

"Can I hold you?" he whispers. "I just want to hold you."

I say nothing. He puts his arms around me and with a firm gentleness pulls me close. I lean into him, clinging to him. We are both sobbing, great convulsive sobs.

"I love you. How could you ever doubt that? I'm lost without you," he says.

"But if you loved me . . . "

How could you? I think, but I can't choke out the words. The vision of Tyler with Shawna enters my mind. I pull away and Tyler pulls me back. In spite of the vision, it feels so natural to be in Tyler's arms . . .

We sit drenching each other with tears, my head on his shoulder, his head on mine. Amber walks past us, slows, then walks on.

"Do you have the car today?" Tyler asks, wiping his face on his shirt sleeve.

I nod.

"Let's go somewhere a little more private."

"Okay," I say, wanting to get away from him and to never leave him, both at the same time.

I drive to the college campus and park at the same spot where Tyler gave me the promise ring.

"I *will* always love you, you know, whether you love me or not," Tyler says, rubbing the ring on his little finger. It looks looser than it did when he put it on earlier this month, when life seemed good.

"How can you *say* that? You love *me* and you're . . . you're . . . *banging* Shawna."

"But I did that *because* I love you."

"What kind of crazy thing is that?" I'm so mad, I'm yelling now. "That's as bad as those creeps who say things like, 'I had to kill her because I loved her so much.'"

"It is not! Can't you listen for once?" Tyler is yelling now, too.

"Okay! Okay! I told you we could talk. So say everything in the world you need to say to me because once we're out of this car, that's it. I never, ever want to see you again!"

"No! You need me as much as I need you! I could tell by the way we held each other! We love each other and that's how things are!"

"How can I love you anymore when I keep seeing your bare butt humping Shawna? In my dreams, when I'm awake, I keep SEEING THAT!" I'm screaming, crying, pounding the steering wheel so hard my hand hurts.

Tyler takes my hand and holds it tight.

"Stop, Lauren. Just listen. Breathe deep. Slow deep breaths," he says. Still, after all this, Tyler can get me calmed down.

"I decided, before I gave you the ring, that I wouldn't pressure you about sex anymore. That I would let it go — not try to make you break any promises to yourself."

"I thought you must really love me then. Most guys wouldn't do that and I thought . . . "

Again, sobs overtake me, the dim-lit vision from the nursery office overtakes me.

"No, but see, that *is* because I love you. No more pressure, as much as I want you, want sex with you, if it's important for *you* to wait, then it's important for *me* to wait."

"But *you* didn't wait!"

"I'm waiting for *you*!"

I turn away from him and look out the window. It is almost as quiet here in the daytime as it is at night. A man on a mountain bike pedals out a driveway at the end of the street, turns onto a walkway that goes over by the frog pond, and then rides out of sight. That's it. Quiet. Nothing happening. Except rumbles of disbelief and confusion within me. That's happening.

"Okay. So you know how important it is for me to try things. You like to be safe, I like to have exciting experiences. Right?"

I nod my head.

"And just because I want to go bungee jumping and you don't, that doesn't mean I don't love you, or that I'm betraying you in any way, does it?"

"God, Tyler! Doing it with Shawna was *not* bungee jumping!"

"No, but see, it was an experience I wanted. I was so sick of being a *virgin*. And I'd rather have had my first sex with you, but I needed it then, not two years down the road."

"So, you decided to love Shawna, instead of me, because she would give you what you wanted?"

"I didn't decide to *love* Shawna. I just decided to have sex with her."

"That's cold. You tricked her into having sex . . . "

"I didn't trick her at all. I didn't tell her I loved her. She doesn't love me."

"If I'd known, Tyler, if you'd told me your plan . . . " I'm caught by crying again.

"No, but see. I didn't want to say, 'If you don't give it to me

I'll go somewhere else for it.' I'm not like that."

"But you *are* like that. You *did* go somewhere else."

"It was just something we both needed to do."

I can't believe my ears. What is he saying? What does he mean?

"I know it sounds strange, but, you know, working together, taking care of plants and all, Shawna and I would talk. And I got to know her. One day we were transplanting some stuff, working in the same area for a long time, and she told me she wished she'd been born a plant."

"A *plant?*"

"Yeah. A plant. Because she thinks plants never get molested by their fathers . . . Remember what she said about her father? And you know he's in prison?"

I nod my head.

"Well, he's in prison because he raped her. And she had the guts to turn him in when her mother was telling her not to."

"God. Why wasn't the mother on Shawna's side?"

"Because the dad was working and he paid the bills . . . Anyway, Shawna thought, because of the rape and all, that maybe she could never, you know, enjoy being with a man. And she wanted to know. And I wanted the experience . . . "

I'm sobbing again and I don't even know why. Is it because of poor Shawna, or because I've lost so much with Tyler, or just because, overall, the world can be such a hard place? Maybe I'm sobbing for the five-year-old girl in Amarillo, Texas, whose mother insisted on staying behind until the girl was rescued. Maybe I'm crying for the blanket that got burned in the fire.

"Don't," Tyler is whispering. "Don't," over and over again and I am sobbing.

"I didn't mean to hurt you. It wasn't a *bad* thing. Shawna always knew I loved *you*. She tried to talk to you . . . "

"But, Tyler . . . "

"I know. It was a shock to see us like that. But I'd have told you. I thought it was a *good* idea. It seemed like it at the time."

We sit in silence, Tyler running his hands through my hair, pulling one curl after another, letting them spring back.

"I want us to get past this," he says. "What can I do?"

"I don't know. I don't know."

"Do *you* want us to get past this?"

"I don't know."

"When I saw the red Honda guy come up that day, all I could think about was how to protect you. I swear, he'd have had to kill me before he could hurt you."

"But if you loved me . . . "

"But I *do* love you. And I'm really sorry you were hurt by this whole thing, but I'm not sorry I did it. It was important to me to have sex. I've had sex. It was nothing like it would have been with you, but it's happened to me, finally, and I'm not sorry."

He tries to pull me close to him but I sit stiffly on my side of the car.

"And Shawna? Is she glad?"

"She said she found out what she needed to know."

"Will you do it again?"

"No. It's done."

"Are you still friends?"

"Yeah. Except she has a different work schedule now that she's at continuation high school."

A rush of shame comes over me.

"It was my fault," I say.

"She likes it there, though."

A group of kids, probably third or fourth graders, come walking down the street carrying a bat and ball. They go down to the very end and start a game of what looks like three flies up. We watch for a long time.

"I should get the car back," I say.

"Can we try to make things right?" Tyler says.

"I'm so confused."

"But can we just try?"

I look into Tyler's eyes. He's never shown anything but love for me. Maybe he *was* trying to do the right thing in backing off from sex with me.

"Can I at least call you later tonight?"

"Yeah, call," I say.

After I drop Tyler off I drive up to the foothills and just sit in the car. I can see the lights coming on in the valley. There are so many people down there who love each other, and hate each other, who forgive and who hold grudges. There are people who are so angry with life they shoot at other innocent people who happen to be driving near them on the freeway. And there are others who will risk their own lives to help a stranger.

Who will I be? Will I go through life hating my mother, hating Baby Hope's mother, hating Tyler for what he's done? Or will I somehow find a way to forgive, so there'll be room in my heart for joy, and love?

There is so much to figure out. I think maybe I *will* try seeing that psychologist Grams told me about. Not that I'm crazy or anything. But it could be good to talk with someone who might help me see things more clearly.

One thing I've figured out on my own, though. I can't put conditions on love. I always thought if my mother loved me, she'd have quit drugs. But then, I find out from my father that she *did* love me, in her own messed-up way, and that I'm alive today because of her love. And I thought if Tyler loved me, he wouldn't have done that with Shawna. But then I think of how he fought Jack when he thought I was in danger, and the look in his eyes when he's with me, and I know he loves me. I don't know if I can ever get the picture of Tyler and Shawna out of my head. And if I can't, I don't know if Tyler and I can work things out. Maybe we can. Maybe we can't.

Finally, I think I can begin to forgive my mother. Maybe Grams can help me, or maybe Jack, or maybe I just have to keep thinking, and writing. I hope it doesn't ruin my volleyball game, but it's worth the risk.

Photo : Melanie Mages

A B O U T

T H E

A U T H O R

In addition to *If You Loved Me,* Marilyn Reynolds is the author of five other young adult novels, *Baby Help, But What About Me?, Too Soon for Jeff, Detour for Emmy,* and *Telling,* and a book of short stories, *Beyond Dreams,* all part of the popular **True-to-Life Series from Hamilton High.**

In addition to her books for teens, Reynolds also has a variety of published personal essays, and was nominated for an Emmy award for the **ABC Afterschool Special,** "Too Soon for Jeff."

Reynolds is a seasoned educator who has worked for more than twenty-five years with teenagers facing a multitude of crises. Her extensive background with young adults includes teaching reluctant learners and at-risk teens at an alternative high school in Southern California. She often is a guest speaker and seminar leader for programs and organizations that serve teens, parents, teachers, and writers.

Reynolds lives in northern California with her husband, Mike. When she is not writing novels or participating in conferences, she enjoys walks along the American River, visits from children and grandchildren, and movies and dinners out.

NOVELS BY MARILYN REYNOLDS
True to Life Series from Hamilton High:

BABY HELP — Melissa doesn't consider herself abused — after all, Rudy only hits her occasionally when he's drinking . . . until she realizes the effect his abuse is having on their child. Finally Melissa leaves Rudy, and she and Cheyenne go to the shelter for battered women. But as difficulties with group living arise, as she misses the good times with Rudy, as Cheyenne points to gray Ford pickups and calls "Daddy," the clarity of Melissa's decision fades and she finds herself again in a dangerous situation, more trapped than ever before.

DETOUR FOR EMMY — Novel about Emmy, pregnant at 15. American Library Association Best Books for Young Adults List; South Carolina Young Adult Book Award.

TOO SOON FOR JEFF — The story of Jeff Browning, a senior at Hamilton High School, a nationally ranked debater, and reluctant father of Christy Calderon's unborn baby. Best Books for Young Adults List; Quick Pick Recommendation for Young Adult Reluctant Reads; ABC After-School TV Special.

BUT WHAT ABOUT ME? — Erica pours more and more of her heart and soul into helping boyfriend Danny get his life back on track. But the more she tries to help him, the more she loses sight of her own dreams. It takes a tragic turn of events to show Erica that she can't "save" Danny, and that she is losing herself in the process of trying.

TELLING — When twelve-year-old Cassie is accosted and fondled by the father of the children for whom she babysits, she feels dirty and confused. *"A sad, frightening, ultimately hopeful, and definitely worthwhile purchase." BookList.*

BEYOND DREAMS — Six short stories dealing with situations faced by teenagers — drinking and driving, racism, school failure, abortion, partner abuse, aging relative.

Visit your bookstore — or order directly from Morning Glory Press
6595 San Haroldo Way, Buena Park, CA 90620. 714/828-1998.
Free catalog on request.
Visit our web site at http://www.morningglorypress.com

ORDER FORM

Morning Glory Press
6595 San Haroldo Way, Buena Park, CA 90620
714.828.1998; 1.888.612.8254   Fax 714.828.2049

			Price	Total
Novels by Marilyn Reynolds:				
__	*Love Rules*	1-885356-76-5	9.95	_____
__	*If You Loved Me*	1-885356-55-2	8.95	_____
__	*Baby Help*	1-885356-27-7	8.95	_____
__	*But What About Me?*	1-885356-10-2	8.95	_____
__	*Too Soon for Jeff*	0-930934-91-1	8.95	_____
__	*Detour for Emmy*	0-930934-76-8	8.95	_____
__	*Telling*	1-885356-03-x	8.95	_____
__	*Beyond Dreams*	1-885356-00-5	8.95	_____
__	Hardcover	1-885356-01-3	15.95	_____
	Breaking Free from Partner Abuse			
__		1-885356-53-6	8.95	_____
	Your Pregnancy and Newborn Journey			
__		1-932538-00-3	12.95	_____
__	*Nurturing Your Newborn*	1-932538-20-8	7.95	_____
__	*Your Baby's First Year*	1-932538-03-8	12.95	_____
__	*The Challenge of Toddlers*	1-932538-06-2	12.95	_____
__	*Discipline from Birth to Three*	1-932538-09-7	12.95	_____
	Teen Dads: Rights, Responsibilities and Joys			
__		1-885356-68-4	12.95	_____
	ROAD to Fatherhood: How to Help Young Dads			
__		1-885356-92-7	14.95	_____
__	*Safer Sex: The New Morality*	1-885356-66-8	14.95	_____
	Teen Moms: The Pain and the Promise			
__		1885356-25-0	14.95	_____
__	Hardcover	1-885356-24-2	21.95	_____
	Teenage Couples: Expectations and Reality			
__		0-930934-98-9	14.95	_____
	— *Caring, Commitment and Change*			
__		0-930934-93-8	9.95	_____
__	— *Coping with Reality*	0-930934-86-5	9.95	_____
__	*Will the Dollars Stretch?* Paper	1-885356-78-1	7.95	_____
__	*Moving On*	1-885356-81-1	4.95	_____

TOTAL _____

Add postage: 10% of total—Min., $3.50; 15%, Canada _____
California residents add 7.5% sales tax _____

TOTAL _____

Ask about quantity discounts, Teacher, Student Guides.
Prepayment requested. School/library purchase orders accepted.
If not satisfied, return in 15 days for refund.

NAME _____ PHONE_____
ADDRESS _____
_____